Another Hamlet

The Mystery of
Leslie Howard

Charles Boyle

Second Edition

Somerville, Massachusetts
2013

Published by

Forever Press
PO Box 263
Somerville MA
www.foreverpress.org

ISBN 978-0-9835027-3-9

Second Edition
©2013, 2011, 1995, 1993

Printed in the USA

Second printing
May 2018
Errata corrected

Dedication

To Jack,

With All My Love

Table of Contents

Introduction to Second Edition   vii

Introduction   ix

To Catch the Conscience of the King   1

Another Hamlet   37

Leslie Howard on Stage   209

Leslie Howard on Film   211

Selected Writing by Leslie Howard   213

Works cited & bibliography   214

Index to names in the essay   225

Index to scenes in the screenplay   229

Introduction to Second Edition

When plans for the first edition of *Another Hamlet* began in 2010 Charles Boyle had just become aware of the publication of the first real biography of Leslie Howard, Estel Eforgan's *Leslie Howard: The Lost Actor* (2010). Some minor changes were made at that time to both the essay and the screenplay based on new information in this book.

In the two years since then public awareness of Leslie Howard has been increasing greatly. There are more internet sites dedicated to him, and a new documentary about him (based in large part on the discovery of many home movies made by Howard himself) will be part of the 75th anniversary release of *Gone with the Wind*.

However, the Oxfordian take on Howard remains mostly unmentioned. A second edition of Eforgan's biography was published earlier this year, and these "Oxford is Shakespeare" scenes and any discussion about them remain off-limits. In an introduction the reader is updated about what's been happening since 2010, but there are (apparently) no changes to the book's original text.

Boyle, however, has decided that his 20-year old screenplay needed to be updated based on what Eforgan had discovered. This second edition contains both an essay and a screenplay that have substantial changes. First, since Eforgan has discovered documents that indicate Howard did not suffer shell-shock in WWI (he was never close to the front) that section of the screenplay has been changed. Second, the fact that Howard had dinner with Mrs. Winston Churchill and several other writers and politicians in winter 1940 during which his upcoming film *Pimpernel Smith* was clearly discussed, a new scene depicting this dinner has been added. Also, several scenes have been added that make it clear that Howard was actively working with his government in collecting information on his cultural trips, especially on his final trip to Portugal and Spain. This theory about Howard remains controversial, and Eforgan, while reporting the facts that support it, does not herself embrace it.

Nonetheless, this theory is clearly a significant part of the discussions of Howard in this re-emergence of his story, a story which is inexorably and forever bound up with the Leslie Howard mystery.

William Boyle
Somerville, Massachusetts
May 2013

Introduction

It's been eighteen years since the essay and screenplay in this book were written. At that time the story of Leslie Howard was still as obscure as it had been in the previous five decades, a strange mystery so mysterious that few even thought of it as a mystery, or thought about Leslie Howard at all. Howard scarcely existed in the public imagination.

Since then much has changed, and in recent years Howard's star has started to rise, and a new generation is learning to appreciate just what a fine actor and a fine human being he was. Just this past year a new book, *Leslie Howard: The Lost Actor* by Estel Eforgan, has appeared. It is the first biography about this award-winning actor written by a non-family member since his death 67 years ago. That is remarkable. One can only wonder why this is so, yet Eforgan herself may have provided an important clue in the section of her book discussing Howard's 1941 film *Pimpernel Smith*. In the twenty plus pages she devotes to the film, Howard's bold promotion of the Earl of Oxford as Shakespeare in two separate scenes is not even mentioned!

In recent years Howard had been starting to emerge from the shadows, and this is most likely due to the frequent mention of his name on the Internet as an outspoken Oxfordian, an attribution based solely on these three scenes in *Pimpernel Smith*. Incredibly, there apparently exists no other extant documentation of his thoughts on the Shakespeare authorship question one way or the other, nor is there any extant discussion, correspondence, etc. about how and why these scenes appear in the popular and critically acclaimed propaganda film. Today an Internet search of Howard will retrieve as many hits with this association as any other, with some heated exchanges about just what these "Oxford" scenes mean.

Based on these scenes alone his name is prominent on Oxfordian websites as one of the "doubters" of the Stratford story. Yet on the Wikipedia entry for *Pimpernel Smith* there is no mention of the "Oxford is Shakespeare" scenes at all. In fact, the one time that someone tried to add this information to the Wikipedia entry for *Pimpernel Smith* (in 2010) it was deleted within a day, and has not since returned. On the other hand, Professor James Shapiro, in his 2010 book on the Shakespeare authorship question *(Contested Will),* notes (194) that these scenes meant that, "The Oxfordian cause had clearly arrived."

Others on the Internet have tried to make the case that these scenes are in fact Howard's attempt to ridicule the anti-Stratfordian position rather than promote it, since his references to Oxford are spoken while he is "fooling" with his Nazi opponents (therefore, they reason, the statement that the Earl of Oxford was Shakespeare must be "foolishness"). Yet anyone who views the entire film can see that the three separate mentions of it really constitute promotion of this idea, not ridicule. Otherwise why mention it at all, let alone three times? Reviews and commentary on *Pimpernel Smith* over the years all point out that Howard's character is "playing the fool" in the name of a higher truth, and is gallant and patriotic in so doing.

It was this aspect of the story (the fool as both truth teller and patriot) that was on Charles Boyle's mind as he delved into what was then known about the life of Leslie Howard (based on the biographies then extant by both his daughter and his son). Charles quickly learned that the world-famous actor of the 1920s and 1930s had by the 1940s become a prominent patriot, and was lionized in his lifetime for his war efforts as a film maker and propagandist for the English cause against the Nazis. He was even rumored to have been a secret agent for his government in these final years.

The past eighteen years have brought some new historical facts to light which help to update the Howard story. In addition to Eforgan's book there was another book on Howard published in 2008 (*El Vuelo de Ibis: Leslie Howard*) in which the Spanish author, José Rey-Xímena, reported that he had interviewed a former co-star and lover of Howard's, Conchita Montenegro, with whom Howard had visited on his ill-fated final trip in spring 1943. She claimed that Howard was indeed on a spy mission for his government, and had secretly met with Franco. Eforgan discusses this in her book (225), and concludes that, while there is no record of a Howard meeting with Franco, it is not implausible.

In fact, Eforgan spends the last section of her book dealing with the various theories about whether Howard was a government agent, and whether or not he—and not Churchill, as some have speculated—was the intended target when his plane was shot down on June 1, 1943, even though British Intelligence (having broken the Enigma Code) apparently knew before hand that the Germans would attack it (as reported in William Stevenson's *A Man Called Intrepid*). The conventional answer to this fact has been that the decoding breakthrough had to be kept secret, and therefore the plane and its passengers had to be sacrificed.

While there are no firm answers to any of these questions, one very interesting fact that Eforgan did uncover is revealed in a letter she reproduces on the very last page (245), but does not incorporate into her narrative. The letter is from a woman, Mavis Batey, who worked as a decoder during the war, and she says in no uncertain terms that protecting the Enigma Code breakthrough would not have been a reason to let the plane go down; she says, citing other examples, a warning could have been issued without tipping off the Germans that the Code was broken. Eforgan, for whatever reason, does not highlight Batey's first-hand point of view about protecting the Enigma Code breakthrough.

The Howard story resonates with the Shakespeare story. He was indeed "another" Hamlet in every way imaginable. And we know about it only because of one work of art—*Pimpernel Smith*. Howard plays the fool and tells the truth; he inserts lines into *Pimpernel* much as Hamlet slipped lines into *The Mousetrap*, and in so doing not only touched the conscience of his audience, but left for posterity the record of what he had done. The lines remain, and each time the movie is replayed, these lines are replayed, repeating the story that "Oxford was Shakespeare." That cannot be a mistake.

William Boyle
Somerville, Massachusetts
March 2011

To Catch the Conscience of the King

An Academy Award may have gone to Laurence Olivier for his portrayal of Hamlet[1], but Leslie Howard, according to his own understanding of the author's identity, may be the only actor who has ever lived out the essence of Hamlet's tragic fate. His is one of the most remarkable untold stories in the history of the English theater.

Though best remembered for the hapless aristocrat he played in Hollywood's ultimate epic, *Gone with the Wind*, the most striking thing about Howard's life was his death. During World War II, while returning from Lisbon on a lecture tour on which his main topic had been An Actor's Approach to Hamlet, the unarmed civilian airliner in which he was traveling was shot down by a squadron of German fighter planes over the Bay of Biscay. His body was never recovered. The mystery surrounding his death has never been fully explained.

"Pimpernel Howard Has Made His Last Trip!" crowed the banner headline in the Nazi newspaper *Der Angriff*, run by Josef Goebbels, Hitler's Minister of Propaganda.[2] They were referring to a film Howard had produced and directed, starring himself, called *Pimpernel Smith* (1941), which was the first and one of the most successful British war films. In this satire of Nazism, he had merciless fun playing a Christ-like hero who constantly outsmarts a gross and humorless villain reminiscent of Dr Goebbels. Continued work like this had, by 1943, earned Howard star billing on the German hit list. William Joyce, the infamous Lord Haw-Haw of Berlin Radio, had long since announced that, upon invasion, "this sarcastic British actor" would be eliminated "along with the Churchill clique."

"Probably no single war casualty has induced in the public of these islands such an acute sense of personal loss," wrote critic C.A. LeJeune. "Howard was more than just a popular actor. Since the war he has become something of a symbol to the British people...he had a passion for England and the English ideal that was almost Shakespearean."

The Germans maintained he was a British Agent on a spy mission though the British just as steadfastly denied it. Some in England claimed it was a case of mistaken identity. Howard's traveling companion bore an unfortunate resemblance to Winston Churchill. That's who the Germans were really after. Sir Winston himself confirms this explanation in his book *The Hinge of Fate*. The

Germans, however, never picked up on it. They finally dismissed the whole incident as merely "an error of judgement."

This mysterious theme of mistaken or masked identity was central to the character of his greatest screen success, the silly English fop who is secretly a savior to aristocrats condemned to the guillotine. It was also the key to his understanding of the author who created Hamlet.

Early on in *Pimpernel Smith* occurs an amusing exchange between Howard and the Goebbels caricature. The smug Nazi declares that Shakespeare was actually a German. Howard considers this possibility for a moment before replying with a charming smile, "How upsetting! Still, you must admit the English translations are remarkable."

This proves to be mere prelude for an announcement Howard will make further along in the story. At the start of another confrontation with his nemesis he holds up a thick volume.

"I've been reading a book," Howard tells him, "that proves conclusively that Shakespeare wasn't really Shakespeare at all. He was the Earl of Oxford. Now, you can't pretend the Earl of Oxford was a German, can you?"

"No."

"There you are."

Later in the scene he adds that, "The Earl of Oxford was a very bright Elizabethan light, but this book will tell you he was a good deal more than that." He again offers it to the German, who declines without a glance.

For anyone who missed the name he repeats it in a subsequent scene set in a cave. Holding a skull he has discovered there, he quotes Hamlet's famous graveyard speech, "Alas, poor Yorick...though she paints her face an inch thick it will come to this." He then turns to the German and informs him, "The Earl of Oxford wrote that."

The insertion of so bold a promotion for a rival Shakespeare was not rare in the British cinema—it was unheard of. One simply didn't do such things. He'd really gone beyond the pale. All his friends looked the other way. Both his son and his daughter in their books on him omit all reference to this heretical idea their father had got hold of.[3] But there it is, repeated twice, in a film conceived, produced and directed by Leslie Howard.

Now the question of who wrote Shakespeare had already been around for a long time, fueled by the Stratford man's remarkable history of absence—no school records, no letters, no manuscripts, the silence when he died—but no one in England had ever advanced their career, to say the least, by making a fuss over it. Still, the case for Oxford, first suggested in 1920 by John Thomas Looney in his book *"Shakespeare" Identified in Edward De Vere, The 17th Earl of Oxford*, has gained a number of sympathetic ears over the years, including James Joyce, Sigmund Freud and, more recently, Supreme Court Justices Henry Blackmun and John Paul Stevens. At the time of his death Leslie Howard, however, was the only member of the British theater establishment to have ever gone public with a dissenting view on this matter. To understand his fierce and particular loyalty to this idea, and the role it played in his strange destiny, one must first understand the idea itself.

The "Shakespeare Problem," as it is commonly called, has been around for nearly two hundred years. It is still with us today. Put in its simplest terms, a succession of noted statesmen and authors, (Whitman, Twain, Herman Melville,[4] Disraeli, Dickens, Bismarck and de Gaulle, among others) have found the Stratford attribution unsupported by any credible evidence beyond the sanction of authority and the weight of tradition. Even his few, odd signatures were attached to documents penned by someone else. It was too much silence, these doubters thought, especially when contrasted with the world of the plays. Henry James wrote that he was "haunted by the conviction that the divine William is the biggest and most successful fraud ever practised on a patient world."

The search for the True Author, like that for the Holy Grail or the Historic Jesus, has led off in many different directions. But since the publication of *"Shakespeare" Identified* dissent has generally coalesced around Oxford.

So who was this man?

Though usually dismissed from conventional English history as a fop and a fool, little better than the man Scarlet Pimpernel pretended to be, Sir Sidney Lee wrote of him:

Oxford, despite his violent and perverse temper, his eccentric taste in dress and his reckless waste of substance, evinced a genuine taste in music and wrote verses of much lyric beauty...Puttenham and Meres [Elizabethan literary men) reckon him among the best for comedy in his day; but though he was a patron of players, *no specimens of his dramatic productions survive*. A sufficient number of his poems is extant to corroborate Webbe's comment, that he was the best of the courtier poets of the early days of Queen Elizabeth, and that 'in the rare devices of poetry he may challenge to himself the title of the most excellent amongst the rest. (*Dictionary of National Biography*. Italics added.)

Perhaps the quickest way to grasp the Oxford theory is to see him as the model for Hamlet, which is how Howard undoubtedly viewed him. Like the hero, he is a prince of the realm, but denied any access to real power (though Oxford dreamt of the kind of military glory achieved by his famous cousins, Francisco and Horatio, the Fighting Veres—the Queen denied him a command), he must content himself with writing and producing plays that attempt to expose the court's corruption (much as Howard attempted to expose what he saw as the Shakespeare Hoax in his own film).

"The players cannot keep counsel—they'll tell all," Hamlet warns the daughter of his would be father-in-law Polonius, now widely recognized as a caricature of Lord Burghley, the most powerful man in England and Oxford's father-in-law.

Since publication of Looney's book, a great deal more has been unearthed about the Earl's once obscure life. Like Ashley Wilkes, he seems to have represented the best and most sensitive in a dying generation of feudal aristocrats, their wealth based on land and family, who was soon to be swept away in the winds of a civil war where the rule of wealth based on capital and incentive would triumph. What Rhett Butler represented in Ashley's world, William Cecil, Lord Burghley, did in Oxford's. Cecil founded his dynasty, which is still very powerful in England today, in large part on the purposeful ruination of his quixotic son-in-law.

Seen in this light, the dilemma becomes self–evident. Shakespeare's plays become political dynamite, the abstracts and brief chronicles of Elizabeth's Court written by the ultimate insider/outsider, a compulsive truth teller in the heart of a national government. What could be worse? The Cecil's could never accept any of this becoming common knowledge. And though the Queen had stood between much heat and that boy, much as Gertrude had Hamlet, how could even she ever reconcile the character of Gertrude with the national myth of a Virgin Queen? For the British Establishment the central issue was not who wrote Shakespeare but what Shakespeare was really writing about. According to this view, he was a problem that touched the Crown. If the plays were to be preserved at all, a plan had to be devised for severing them from political reality. Eventually this involved setting up the Stratford man like Woody Allen in *The Front*, as a cover for the true author. And the works themselves would thus become history's most famous "purloined letter."

Oxford, it is suggested, acquiesced to this necessity though it left him heartbroken, to realize the price he had paid for his license was the anonymity of Lear's Fool. "My name be buried where my body is..." as the author laments in sonnet 74.

His family and friends knew their duty. There was nothing to gain and everything to lose in openly challenging the official version. Perhaps a wild boy like Marlowe was assassinated under the guise of a barroom brawl because he knew too much and couldn't be trusted. As in Howard's day, Elizabethan writers were often employed as spies and became privy to much secret information.

And once something like this is set in motion, how can it be stopped? Admitting to it would seem to legitimize a veritable Pandora's Box of conspiracy theories touching the Crown, everything from "Who killed the little Princes?" to "Who was Jack the Ripper?" to "What did Rudolf Hess know?" No, if the Shakespeare Problem began as a national security issue, then it must remain one, even if only in terms of not breaking the faith.

This solution would then be the cause for what T.S. Eliot termed our "semi-mythical Shakespeare."

Certainly this theory lends added poignancy to Hamlet's dying words to his most trusted friend,

> "Oh God, Horatio, what a wounded name, things standing thus unknown, shall live behind me. If thou didst ever hold me in thy heart, absent thee from felicity awhile, and in this harsh world draw thy breath in pain, to tell my story."

Not coincidentally, Pimpernel Smith's first name is Horatio.[5]

Leslie Ruth Howard wrote in her book, *A Quite Remarkable Father*, that the role of Hamlet was "a lifetime's ambition" for her father. And indeed, much that is mysterious and paradoxical in this most famous of all literary creations appears mirrored in her father's remarkable life.

Though regarded by millions as the ideal Englishman, Howard was actually the first born son of a Hungarian Jew and the British girl he took for his bride. He was born into the hub of the British Empire at its height—London, 1893—and spent a relatively happy childhood in and around this world capital, protected from a rather stern and remote father by his adoring and indulgent mother. Working as a bank clerk when the Great War broke out, he immediately enlisted in a British cavalry regiment. Just before he was sent to France he met and married Ruth Martin, who remained his devoted wife for the rest of his life. A steady, down–to earth woman, she would act, much like Gertrude, as a shield for her rather vague and ethereal young man against a harsh world with which he bore the most tenuous rapport. Howard would rely on her strength throughout his career, right from the start.

For though the War had rescued him from the suffocating regime of the banking world it had sent him back severely disillusioned and depressed. Ruth nursed him through his recovery. But after that the thought of returning to life as a bank clerk was unbearable. He now found the courage to approach his true love, the world of the theater, the only world where Hamlet ever found joy.

"As a boy the possibility of being an actor never even occurred to me," he would later write. "Nor could it have occurred to anybody who knew the shy and inarticulate youth that I was. I wanted to write. I felt I could express myself on paper; alone in a room I felt articulate and creative." For the rest of his life he dreamed of fame as a writer.

While still a schoolboy he wrote his first play— in Latin. After that, however, he wrote only in English. He published his first story in a penny dreadful called, appropriately enough, *The Penny Magazine*. "The Impersonation of Lord Dalton, A Story of the Diplomatic Service," as he called it, followed the adventures of a forger pressed into service by the British Foreign Office to impersonate a nobleman on a spy mission, eventually proving himself and wedding a lovely titled lady. Already some of the key themes in Howard's life were sounded, including mistaken or masked identity in the worlds of espionage and the nobility.

Among his later plays his personal favorite was called *Willie* (incidentally an affectionate nickname for Shakespeare). This title character he described as "the silly ass Englishman par excellence" who was, of course secretly, in reality, the Black Knight, a glamorous highwayman. Needless to say, this dark knight foreshadowed his most popular role, the Scarlet Pimpernel.

In fact, throughout his career Howard excelled at playing doomed intellectuals and high-born gentleman leading double lives. In one film he was cast as a British agent, in another a waiter mistaken for a prince. In the book *Tales From the Hollywood Raj* he is described as "visibly a poet and a dreamer, perfectly typecast in *Outward Bound* as a man already beyond the grave and belonging therefore to some other world."

In this world he was known as something of a tightwad with his funds, though unusually generous with his talent. While playing the failed artist and crippled medical student in *Of Human Bondage* he was warned that Bette Davis, still a relatively unknown contract player at Warner Brothers, would steal the film if he wasn't careful. "If I am very careful," he replied, "She will steal the picture." Her electrifying performance opposite him turned her into a star. Humphrey Bogart had already failed in films and was resigned to playing dull studs on the New York stage when Howard picked him out to play the gangster against his world weary writer in *The Petrified Forest*. The role made Bogart. Howard, having promised him he would play it again in the movie version, refused to sign without him. Bogart was so grateful he named one of his children Leslie.

Still, despite all his success and popularity, Howard was considered something of a lightweight. All his training and experience had been in romantic comedies and dramas, mostly trifles, where he had been among the first of a new breed of actors who, heeding the advice of Hamlet to his players to "hold as it `twer the mirror up to nature," had brought a more natural playing style to the English stage after World War I. The now distant world of high drama was foreign to him. Perhaps because he made acting look so easy it was assumed that until he tackled Shakespeare he hadn't really proven himself. Ironically he had starred as the Bard himself in a 1933 London production of a play called *This Side Idolatry* but had not yet appeared in a Shakespearean play.[6]

"We do wonder why it is that Mr. Howard has never bothered to enlarge his field," he read about himself in the newspaper one morning. "Or to play the truly courageous part in the theater which could so easily be his." And this, further down, he marked in blue pencil: "...it leaves one wondering why a man who ought to make an interesting Hamlet...should have elected to be so unadventurous as an actor."

Howard took up the gauntlet. He not only began preparations for a New York production of *Hamlet* but when Irving Thalberg offered him the role of Romeo opposite Norma Shearer's Juliet in a lavish film version of that play, he accepted, finding in Romeo "a baby Hamlet." "One may, therefore, understand," he added. "Why an actor who has ambitious designs upon the Danish prince and who has never spoken a word of Shakespeare, should want to take his first classical steps in this part." The resulting film was received respectfully enough though everyone in the cast looked too old for their roles.

Howard continued planning for his *Hamlet*. In doing so he attempted to avoid the extremes of either anything-for-an-effect radicals or the hide-bound traditionalists by steering a course straight "to Shakespeare as one man of the theater to another," adding, "I have had the nerve to consider the two of us co-workers in a theatrical enterprise and have tried to forget that my partner is separated from me by over three hundred years of time...."

As producer he spared no expense on this production. A first rate supporting cast was assembled. With his generous eye for unknowns he had even offered the role of Ophelia to a yet to be discovered Vivian Leigh, but she was waiting on a film offer in London and became unavailable. Agnes de Mille was engaged to do the choreography, Virgil Thomson the music. John Houseman would co-direct with Howard. The sets, the costumes, everything was magnificently prepared. Word of this coming *Hamlet* aroused great anticipation in New York. Indeed, it was destined to be the talk of the 1936 season, that famous year when two Hamlets ran on Broadway. And there was the rub.

John Gielgud, the premier classical actor of his generation, accepted an offer to bring his *Hamlet* to town that same season. Howard, somewhat shocked, wondered why a rival *Hamlet* should have been so suddenly introduced into this, his great adventure in the role. Some even suggested it was done on purpose, just to upstage this "upstart crow" of a movie star. Whatever the reason, it was too late to turn back. While he received promising notices out of town—"...a natural Hamlet," "...a beautifully repressed Hamlet," and "one of these days...Leslie Howard too will be looked back upon as a great Hamlet"—his reviews in New York were not as good.

Houseman had begged his star not to go head to head against Gielgud. My God, he had been working on his *Hamlet* for over ten years! Tour, let the production mature, and then come back after Gielgud had got out of town. Sound advice no doubt but Howard, perhaps believing that a second gauntlet had been thrown down, refused to listen. He seemed to treat it all as destined. He was, Houseman later wrote, "the most completely fatalistic man I had ever met." Nervous, tired, distracted, he opened in New York on schedule. It was a disaster. It may possibly go down as the most famous failed *Hamlet* of the century. Almost without exception the critics savaged him. This, from John Anderson, was typical:

> To say that Mr. Howard is a pleasant actor, a charming fellow, with few equals at the lightly romantic stuff he has become famous for explains his popularity as a figure in the theater without offering any reason why he should undertake one of the theater's great roles.

John Mason Brown called it *"Hamlet* with the Hamlet left out," and, in one of the most popular sallies of the day, let Gielgud know he was free to drop the Giel from his name as his was "the Gud Hamlet."

Not that he didn't have his defenders. The critic for *Cue Magazine* wrote, "Vicious, critical attacks to the contrary, this department thinks the Howard Hamlet is in no way less distinguished than the other, although it apparently came as a shock to the Gielgud-conditioned critical gentry."

Soon everyone had an opinion and it became the sport of New York to compare the two Hamlets. Serious theatergoers didn't want to miss either one. Gielgud recalled cabbies asking him, "Which Hamlet are you?" The general consensus came to be that his volatile and unpredictable Prince dominated the stage while Howard's elusive, self-effacing intellectual was less than overwhelming.

This ill-fated *Hamlet* proved to be Howard's swan song to the stage. From now on he would concentrate on film.

Howard had always been more a cinematic than theatrical actor anyway—Burns Mantle called him "one of the drama's most eloquent listeners"—but he was frustrated by more than the problems of stage projection, he was frustrated by acting itself. He had always regarded it as a somewhat silly profession for a man and, like the author of the Sonnets, was rather chagrined to have made himself a "motley to the view."

He continued to dream of fame as a writer and had already published a number of humorous sketches on show business in *The New Yorker* and *Vanity Fair*. During the Twenties, while living on Long Island, he had many long discussions on the mysteries of playwriting with his neighbor and fellow aspiring dramatist, F. Scott

Fitzgerald. One of Howard's plays had even made it to Broadway. But nothing came of it. Now he produced another in England, *Alias Mrs. Jones* [written by him], attacking the unlimited power of the press barons to suppress and control the news, a theme rich with Oxfordian vibrations. That vanished too. He decided the cinema was the thing wherein to catch the conscience of a mass audience. A film, after all, would always be there. As long ago as the early 20's, when he was practically unknown, Howard had helped create Minerva Films, dedicated to bringing distinctive British comedies to the screen.[7] But they could only afford two reelers and soon went broke. Now he saw how he could trade on his tremendous popularity as a world class star to revive his real ambition of getting movies made that he wanted to make.

He began to develop scripts for ideas that appealed to him, many of which seemed resonate with the Oxford/Hamlet mystery. One concerned "Bonnie Prince Charlie" of Scotland, the Young Pretender to the Throne of England. He had always been attracted to, as his daughter put it, "that rather touching, romantic figure, and his forlorn hope."

Another had come to him while visiting the Isle of Wight to see the airplane that was to win the Schneider Trophy for Great Britain. He noticed a familiar looking man quietly polishing the soon to be famous plane. He looked again. It couldn't be.

"Is that...?" he asked his military host.

"Yes, you're right. Aircraftman Shaw—the extraordinary Lawrence of Arabia."

"So that's Lawrence...what a strange fellow he is—after what his life has been, to spend his days polishing an airplane...odd."

The strange fate of this distinctly English hero, who of his own volition had spiraled down from world fame to total oblivion, fascinated him. Knowing he would be ideally suited to the part he determined then and there to make a film about Lawrence, who had wondered in his book *The Seven Pillars of Wisdom* "if all established reputations were founded, like mine, on fraud."

Howard may have communicated some of his enthusiasm for Lawrence to the young film editor on his next project for eventually David Lean did make a film about the mysterious Aircraftman Shaw.

This next project, following fast on the heels of the *Hamlet* debacle and two Hollywood comedies in which he played respectively a Shakespearean actor (*It's Love I'm After)* and a movie producer

11

(*Stand-in)*[8], was a film version of George Bernard Shaw's *Pygmalion*.[9]
It was be a turning point in his life.

First of all, to secure his services as star, the producer, Gabriel
Pascal, had agreed to let Howard co-direct the movie with the witty
Anthony Asquith. This was the opportunity he had been hungering
for. In Hollywood such an arrangement would have been next to
impossible but in England things were different. (However, he would
exert exactly this same blackmail again, signing to play Ashley
Wilkes—a role he detested in a book he never read—only after a
desperate David Selznick agreed to make him associate producer on
Intermezzo.[10]

And again George Bernard Shaw's story of an upperclass person
who must pass off a lower class person as a Duchess by instructing
her in the art of language touched on Oxfordian themes of deception
and identity that had intrigued him since he was a boy.

But, most importantly, on the set of *Pygmalion* he met a young
woman who would change his life.

The fact is deception had been a bigger part of Howard's life than
his public ever suspected. His career had been a relatively smooth rise
from obscurity to stardom, his image that of a noble and charming
hero who was also a devoted father and the perfect husband. In reality
he had been living a double life for years.

In his book, *In Search of My Father*, Ronald Howard describes his
famous father as "a rather over-romantic schoolboy...torn between
opposites," comparing him to Ashley in *Gone with the Wind*. On the
one hand he had his Melanie, the devoted, adoring and long suffering
Ruth, and on the other a dizzying succession of Starlets, mostly
actresses, with whom he shared ephemeral and idle allied romances,
conducted with such tact and discretion that there was never a breath
of scandal. Though these liaisons seemed to come and go with the
roles he played, flashing out as quickly as the kiss of fire to
gunpowder, they may have given him the spark that made him a star.

His most explosive affair so far had been with the actress who
played his wife in *The Scarlet Pimpernel*, Merle Oberon. Like him,
she was only half-English, yet she shared his passionate love of
England. She may well have engaged in some Intelligence activities
herself during the war, and is said to have been in Lisbon when she
learned of Howard's death. At the height of their affair he had been so
madly in love that he flew through a blizzard to Hollywood a few

days before opening *The Petrified Forest* in New York, an uncertain flight in those days, just to find one night of inspiration with her.

Though it seemed for awhile that they might marry the affair ended during the long run of that play. Unromantically, Howard came down with a terrible case of boils. One of them, planted comically on his nose, might have killed him since there is a nasal vein near that spot that leads directly to the brain. In spite of this he dragged himself to every performance. But Merle soon discovered that in his acute embarrassment and distress he would only accept his wife's care.

All that changed on the set of *Pygmalion* when he met Violette Cunnington, personal assistant to Gabriel Pascal. If he had found his Gertrude in Ruth, Violette was his Juliet. "Like the figure fashioned by Pygmalion," his son wrote. "She would become his image of perfect love...a love that was to last five years to the end of her very short life."

She was twenty-four when they met, he forty-five. By the end of production he had persuaded her to come work for him. Soon they had fallen deeply in love. Yet Howard could not give up his family for her. Certainly Ruth had always been something of a mother to him, the mainstay of his turbulent emotional life. But now he found that, unlike his other loves, he couldn't let Violette go.

"We tried to crush it all at birth..." he later wrote. "For not long after, doubting me, you went away to France. And I, from pride or stupidity—or perhaps from fear—let you go. And as you went I knew my life was in the aeroplane with you."

They were reunited and his double life resumed in earnest. He never sought a divorce. Ruth endured even this but now, clearly, Violette was the vital element in his life. Once again his films reflected his life. After *Gone With The Wind* he made his last American movie, *Intermezzo*, in which he played a married violinist who falls in love with his young protégée. It was a lovely romance but not one with a happy ending.

In the summer of 1939, knowing war was imminent, he returned to England, to be joined separately by both family and mistress. He had plans to direct and act in a film based on the novel, *The Man Who Lost Himself*, by H. de Vere Stacpoole.[11] The plot revolves around a commoner who must switch identities with a nobleman, who then dies, leaving the imposter to live out his troubled life. "What quite attracted Leslie to the story," his son wonders. "I do not know..."

That fall Hitler attacked Poland, England declared war and the world was changed forever. Yet in those first few months that the English called "the phoney war" little appeared to happen. "I feel rather like Stacpoole's hero," Howard wrote his son. "But lost in a more than fictional sense and I am beginning to wonder why I am here and what I am doing here."

Financing for his film fell through. In fact all of English feature film production ground to a halt. Such endeavors appeared frivolous in light of the current crisis. Yet no one in the business seemed to have a clear idea as to how to proceed. Indeed, very few were even interested. Howard, frustrated by the inertia and anxious to be of use, cast about in his mind for a suitable project. He remembered a brief holiday trip he'd made to Austria just before Hitler's Anschluss in January 1938. While there he had met Alfons Walde, a painter, who invited him to his studio. There, privately, he told Howard that Austria was finished. It was only a matter of time before Hitler crossed the border. He spoke of friends who had disappeared already in Germany. He glanced about the room at his expressionist paintings. Too free, too decadent, too Jewish. Dr. Goebbels would never stand for this. "I have many good friends here," he said. "But within weeks we'll have new masters—and, then...it will be a little unstable..."

Howard wondered now about his fate and the fate of thousands like him. The germ of an idea began to grow in his mind. As his daughter described it, "...the setting should be Austria in 1938; a famous painter, who was also a violent anti-Nazi, is arrested by Hitler's thugs. He must be saved somehow..."

All through the early part of 1940 he worked on an outline for this story, bringing in other writers until the screenplay was satisfactory. But the real problem was finding the money. For over a year Howard went hat in hand to one prospective backer after another, feeling like a traveling salesman, trying to sell his idea. But the British film industry remained moribund and unresponsive to commercial production. Everything now was geared towards the war. Howard agreed that film entertainment would be nothing more "than a trivial occupation where there remained such tremendous and historic tasks to be done" unless its powerful potential for propaganda were exploited.

At this point another aspect of the Oxford story becomes relevant. In 1586 the Queen gave him a grant of one thousand pounds a year—fully one per cent of the national budget—to be paid him out of Secret Service funds. As was customary with such funds, Oxford never had to account for a penny of it. He spoke of his "office" in a letter to the Lord Treasurer of England but no record of that office has come down to us. There was, however, a rumor then current in England that Shakespeare spent at the rate of a thousand pounds a year.

Oxford's whole life had been spent deeply immersed in theatrical and publishing activities. A circle of writers gathered around him, including Anthony Munday, Robert Greene, Thomas Watson, John Lyly and Christopher Marlowe. He was patron to not one but several theater companies.

Around the time of his extraordinary grant a sudden, unprecedented outpouring of plays, pamphlets and poems began to appear in England, many unabashedly meant to stir the populace into a patriotic fervor against the threat of the Spanish Armada. Even a play like *Othello* could be seen as political allegory, the insanely jealous Moor standing for Spain and Desdemona the Protestant Low Lands underfoot—such would life be under Spanish domination.

"Shakespeare," Keats once declared, "lived a life of allegory and his plays are the comments upon it." To those, like Howard, who believe Oxford was the Bard, this amazing Golden Age of Literature didn't just happen, it was made to happen, financed by the British Treasury and guided by the hand of Shakespeare. He was, in a manner of speaking, their first Minister of Propaganda.

Now, during another battle for Britain, Leslie Howard began doing a series of broadcasts for the BBC to alert his adopted country across the sea to the danger of letting Europe fall to the Nazis. In the summer of 1940 France collapsed so suddenly it left a hush. England seemed doomed. This was the atmosphere in which Howard wrote and delivered his first broadcast to America:

> Most of you, I'm sure, will know what I mean when I speak of the curious elation which comes from sharing in a high and mysterious destiny. The destiny of Britain we cannot know for certain, but we can guess at it and pray for it, and work towards it as we find ourselves singled out of all the nations of the world for the rare honor of fighting alone against the huge and ruthless forces of tyranny.

All through those grim, uncertain days he continued to remind his listeners that "the happiest peoples in the civilized world today," were like *Henry V's* "...few, we happy few, we band of brothers," fearlessly waging the good fight against terrorism, domination and lies. His was Shakespeare's message again. Finally British National Films saw the virtue in a modern Pimpernel, this one rescuing commoners from the Gestapo. After all, even the original film had been seen by its makers as a warning against political fanaticism on the Continent, with Shakespeare's "This England," speech, delivered by Howard, inserted at the close to drive the point home.

On April 2,1940, Harold Nicholson, then parliamentary secretary at the Minister for Information, wrote in his diary:

> Dine with Kenneth Clark. Willie (Somerset) Maugham, Mrs Winston Churchill and Leslie Howard were there. We have an agreeable dinner and talked mostly about films. Leslie Howard was doing big propaganda film and is frightfully keen about it. We discuss the position of those English people who had remained over in the United States. The film star claimed that they had been asked to remain there since they were more useful in Hollywood, but we all regret bitterly that people like Aldous Huxley, Auden and Isherwood should have absented themselves ... I come back to Leslie Howard and he continued to talk excitedly about his new film. He seemed to enter into such things with a zest of a schoolboy and that was part of his charm.[12]

The film he was talking about was *Pimpernel Smith*. We will get back to this evening a little later.

In the late fall of 1940 an agreement was signed to begin filming an updated version, with the star to act as producer and director.

During this time the flat Howard and Violette shared in London was hit by German bombs. "A great gaping hole had been blown in the building and the iron window frames had been torn out like so much paper and lay twisted in the courtyard," as he described the scene to his radio audience. "One bomb had fallen on the street where we had stood the day before. I looked at the wreckage fascinated, for the bomb had hit the exact spot where we had taken refuge."

Still, for awhile, their life together continued. On week-ends he would return to his country home to visit his family. But Violette sensed that the best now lay behind them. Those had been their last days in California, while he had been making *Gone with the Wind* and *Intermezzo* and they had been able to escape alone together out into the desert.

"There were out of the eight months five at least of a joyous and rare perfection," he later wrote. "Of an awareness of the beauty of life that neither had known before. Long after, in a gray winter of war, you said wistfully: 'Those five months were the peak. We shall never have anything like that again.' And I argued—'Of course we will. One day we shall go back, we shall recapture them.' But you insisted: 'No, no— they are gone forever.'"

They worked together on his various projects. She even took the small role of the gift shop assistant in *Pimpernel Smith*.

When this film, the first feature shot in England since the war began, was finally released it proved to be enormously popular and influential. Raoul Wallenberg saw it and confided in his sister that someday he would like to emulate its hero. Ironically, the thousand he eventually rescued from the Nazis were the people of Howard's father, the Jews of Hungary.[13]

It also inspired Noel Coward to make *In Which We Serve* and he asked Howard to speak the prayer to fallen sailors that concludes the film. Howard then made a brief appearance in *The 49th Parallel*, another propaganda film about a U-boat crew attempting to escape across Canada, to deliver a ringing denunciation of Nazi lies that was aimed straight at Josef Goebbels by name.

He played himself in *From the Four Corners*, showing three Commonwealth soldiers around London and stressing its heritage as the center of the Empire. Then, while producing and directing a documentary about women in the service called *The Gentle Sex*, he began the long and difficult task of shooting *The First of the Few* on location under wartime conditions.

This film, which he also produced and directed, was about R.J. Mitchell, the doomed, unassuming man who had developed the Spitfire fighter plane. (It had been one of Mitchell's earlier planes that Howard had seen Aircraftman Shaw polishing on the Isle of Wight.) The Spitfire, like Drake's fleet against the Armada, had proved more maneuverable than the enemy craft and was instrumental in winning the Battle of Britain. Noel Coward later remarked to a friend that Howard's performance of this tragic figure was "acting that transcended acting."

Like Prince Hal, he had risen above the expectation of the world. No longer a lightweight, he was now considered something of a national symbol, having come to embody not only the sense of honor and duty but the flair for humor and defiance in the British spirit.

His last public appearance in London was as Lord Nelson in a patriotic pageant on the steps of St Paul's that commemorated Trafalgar Day. He chose to close the show with the war hero's last prayer before the battle that ended Napoleon's dream of invading England. His son also notes that it was in this legendary action off the coast of Spain that Nelson too was felled by a sniper's bullet.

Shortly after this appearance Howard took to bed with a bad cold brought on by overwork. While Violette was nursing him she developed a small red sore on her nose. He soon recovered but she continued to grow worse. The mysterious infection spread remorselessly. Doctors were called in, medicines proscribed. All to no avail. She was taken to a hospital where, within a week, she died in her sleep of cerebral meningitis.

Howard was completely stunned by the sudden death of his Juliet. He blamed everyone—the doctors, the nurses, the constricting family he cherished, but most of all he blamed himself and cursed his own selfish nature. He had driven them both to hard, asked too much, far too much, of her. Yet this undoubtedly had been the most intense relationship he had ever known. His grief was not only like Romeo's, in the uncanny manner his life had of being reflected in his films, it also echoed another character he had played years ago, a man whose fiancee dies on the eve of their wedding (*Smilin' Through*, 1932). He spends the remainder of his life remembering her and awaiting each evening for her spirit to return.

"What is the mystery of our coming together...?" he would write. "We can never, never part—it was not just for nothing."

Like Hamlet, Howard was now haunted by a ghost of his own. He became increasingly involved in spiritualism, discovering among some of Violette's friends those who could teach him the delicate arts of automatic writing and the planchette system. He even attended some seances. "Leslie spent hours seated at his desk," his son reports,

Composing messages to Violette and, apparently, receiving replies...Leslie firmly believed that whatever actions or decisions he took were, in the mysterious ways of such beliefs, directly due to these communications...as if he were receiving direct advice and guidance from Violette.

Always of a highly mystical bent of mind, he now became even more so. She was forever in his thoughts. "Very quickly after you left me you took hold of my consciousness..." he wrote. "And you aroused in me a sense beyond my physical senses, an inner sense of seeing, hearing, feeling. You made me know, beyond all doubt, that there is no death; that man, above all things, is a spirit – that the spirit once created is indestructible."

He himself had only seven months to live.

Slowly he returned to his film work, producing another propaganda documentary, this one celebrating nurses, called *The Lamp Still Burns*. And he picked up plans for his next major project, a contemporary film version of *Hamlet*.

It was to be set in war-torn Denmark with himself in the title role. He saw parallels between his time and Hamlet's everywhere. Once again the country was on a war-footing, only now it was Hitler rather than Fortinbras who threatened invasion. Claudius, who had usurped the throne, stood for Quisling-style collaborator governments. And the Prince, in Howard's mind, was the embodiment of the national resistance, rising to rid the land of evil misrule. Though he was passionate about making this film he again found money for it hard to come by. He had tried to interest the British Council in his idea.

"As a war film?" came the incredulous reply. "Hamlet's a loser, Leslie. He dies. We're going to live and win! It's bad propaganda material."

They did, however, now approach him to undertake a lecture tour of Portugal and Spain, ancient enemy from the Armada days. At first he demurred, claiming he wasn't the right person for this kind of thing [Violette also warned him against traveling outside England]. But the Council persisted. At this point in the war, with a European invasion still more than a year off, the continued neutrality of Spain had become a delicate matter. Franco was still both fascist and pro-German, so Gibraltar still might fall. It was of vital interest to the British High Command that Spain remain out of the war. Popular actors like Howard, whom the Spanish adored, were needed to advance the Allied viewpoint against the reams of Nazi propaganda issuing from Madrid. Still Howard balked. He'd heard there was still tremendous anti-British feeling there and he didn't want to become a lightening rod for it. After all, he was famous for despising Nazis. It was known he was a marked man. Why tempt fate? How much difference could one lecture tour make?

At this point Anthony Eden, later the Earl of Avon, intervened. Secretary of state for foreign affairs during the war and second only to Churchill in the British Government, Eden interceded for the British Council and finally persuaded Howard to undertake the journey. Under the circumstances one can only imagine he had given him something more to do than lecture. Eden's letter to Howard in the spring of 1943 shows how determined he was that Howard make this trip.[14]

Provisional reservations on the civilian flight to Lisbon were made for him and Alfred Chenhalls, a partner in his film company and the man who would be said to look like Churchill. But complications arose and their departure had to be delayed.

The next day Howard noticed a headline chalked on a news-vendor's board—"British Civil Air-Liner Attacked!" He asked Chenhalls about it at dinner that night. Where had it happened?

"Somewhere in the Bay of Biscay—off Portugal," his jovial friend replied, then adding quickly, "The plane landed safely in Lisbon. It couldn't have been very serious—nobody got a scratch."

Howard wondered if it was the same flight on which they'd been booked. Chenhalls shrugged and offered him some champagne. "I don't think they were gunning for us, old boy!" he winked.

In fact the attacked plane, the *Ibis*, was the same plane on which the two men would die a few weeks later. It was the only plane on the Lisbon run that would be lost to enemy fire during the entire war.

Two days before he finally did leave Howard had a private dinner with Anthony Eden.[15] Nothing is recorded of their meeting but men generally discuss their work. They must have reviewed his lecture plans.

The backbone of his talk was to be seven soliloquies he had selected from *Hamlet*. In his son's words, they "emphasized its extraordinary timelessness, it's then and now sense, which made it contemporary with the current world scene." One in particular referred to an impending battle for a "little patch of ground" that was to be defended to the death by it's garrison. Dover Wilson, whom Howard was using for a guide, thought it relevant to the defense of some sand dunes near Ostend in 1601 by Sir Francis Vere against the Spaniards— "two thousand souls" pitted against "the twenty thousand men" of Spinola's army—fighting "for a plot whereon the numbers cannot try the cause, which is not tomb enough and continent to hide the slain."

Howard had carefully underlined the fate of this predominantly Spanish army that "for a fantasy and trick of fame go to their graves like beds."

The parallel to Gibraltar could not have been lost on his audience. And privately Howard must have thought that here, discreetly, his own Oxford/Hamlet, Edward De Vere, was saluting a famous victory won by one of his illustrious cousins. The soldier standing watch when the play opens is named Francisco.

Perhaps he tried to interest Eden in supporting his *Hamlet* project, even if Hamlet was a loser. (Not long afterwards, Laurence Olivier, ever practical where Howard was quixotic, hit upon the definitive Shakespearean winner and produced, with full government support, his magnificent film version of *Henry the Fifth*.) And then, perhaps, he had even tried to interest Eden in Oxford himself. If so, it would be interesting to know what response he got. It has been said that Winston Churchill, when offered a copy of *"Shakespeare" Identified*, turned it down cold with the remark, "I don't like to have my myths tampered with."[16]

In any event Ruth has always remembered his last words to her. "I don't know why," he said at the gate of the Tudor home they had restored together, "but I have a queer feeling about this whole trip. Still, what the hell!"

With that he was off, flying uneventfully to Lisbon on the ill-fated *Ibis*.

In retrospect it all seemed hauntingly prophetic. "He became like the visitor from another planet," wrote one who was there. "He had a strange mystical quality that...enabled him...to make an impact on men and women in a tragic evocative sense."

"We saw a new Hamlet," added another, "...original and unmistakable—a Hamlet-Howard. He gave us...an unforgettable performance, in the profoundly poetic voice of Shakespeare, of the collective spirit of England."

The layers of meaning which reverberated in his life magnified the shock of his death. Many strange omens were recalled. A flamenco dancer had refused to perform after claiming she saw the skull inside the movie star's face. Twice in Spain he had sat down to a table laid for thirteen. There were thirteen passengers on the last flight. One of them told his wife he had dreamt the plane would be shot down with him in it but failed to cancel his flight for fear of looking foolish. Another confided to a friend, "I'm not normally frightened but somehow I feel bad about this air—trip. I wish I could go to sleep here and wake up at some English airfield."

Howard himself suffered from an eerie recurrent dream which he described to a friend. "Someone with a message for me.... In this dream a dead person is trying to tell me something important—and I cannot understand what it is."

One Father Holmes was called off the *Ibis* at the last minute before take-off by a message to receive a mysterious phone call which he was never able to trace. Thus his life was spared. Some say the call came from God, others from a more earthly but, in this instance, equally well-informed source.[17]

In her book, written fifteen years after his death, Howard's daughter dismisses all such superstitious notions along with any idea that her father was a spy.

But his son, writing another fifteen years later, is willing to concede that Howard may very well have been involved in espionage. He interviewed an English officer who swore he'd met Leslie Howard in Gibraltar during May of 1943 when he had supposedly traveled only to the capital. While in Madrid Howard had met with an attractive young woman described by Ian Colvin in *Flight 777* as "the daughter of a small Argentine farmer...(who) played extra parts in Hollywood and then...met a Belgian who seemed to offer her security until this German Count came along touring America..." They married and settled in Berlin as the war clouds gathered. Now traveling alone and known as "the Countess," she may have been, like Ophelia, a wavering spy he was attempting to "turn." He wrote her from Lisbon, hoping "she would be able to reach England soon."

On the news of Howard's death she went to the Films Director at the British Council in Madrid and "sank to the floor sobbing and confessed that she was an enemy agent who had been specially charged to watch the movements of the film star in the Spanish capital...she swore she had never meant to harm him. Others of her service had been acting similarly in Portugal, she said, and she passionately blamed them for his death."

Howard's daughter supports a theory that the rotund, cigar chomping Alfred Chenhalls was mistaken by German agents in Lisbon for Winston Churchill. The Prime Minister was known to be in Algiers at this time, conferring with his military commanders and Anthony Eden. In his book, *The Hinge of Fate*, he wrote:

Eden and I flew home by Gibraltar. As my presence in North Africa had been fully reported, the Germans were exceptionally vigilant, and this led to a tragedy which much distressed me. The regular commercial aircraft was about to start from the Lisbon airfield when a thickset man smoking a cigar walked up and was thought to be a passenger on it. The German agents therefore signaled that I was on board...a German war plane was instantly ordered out, and the defenseless aircraft was ruthlessly shot down. (p. 742)

Howard's son does not find this explanation entirely credible. He points out, as does Churchill himself, that the Germans would have to be pretty stupid to think the Prime Minister of England would return home on an unescorted civilian airliner in broad daylight in the middle of a war. Besides, it was the Germans who broke the news of the attack and correctly identified both Howard and Chenhalls as being among the missing in their first reports. Nevertheless this story persists to this day and was even repeated in a TV documentary in the 1950s about Churchill's war years.

The Germans had tried a mistaken identity theory of their own, unremembered now, perhaps because they lost the war. Their claim was that the *Ibis*, plainly marked and flying on a scheduled run through clear skies, had appeared to be a military aircraft. When that wouldn't fly they finally dismissed the whole thing as an unfortunate accident, rather as Claudius was prepared to do on the death of Hamlet.

And this is how Howard's son suspects it was. His father was killed through an act of intentional murder.

In the book, *A Man Called Intrepid*, by William Stevenson, one final, very English twist is revealed:

A doubly tragic incident was the killing of Leslie Howard. He boarded an aircraft on a secret mission .... The Germans knew about it and shot down the unarmed plane. The British knew beforehand that the Germans knew, but to protect the secret of how they knew (they had broken the German code), British Intelligence, which had monitored the German Air Force orders, let the plane go down.[18]

In 1576 Oxford was attacked by pirates while crossing the Channel home to England. Hamlet too was attacked by pirates while making the same crossing. And that's pretty much how Leslie Howard died.

The "divinity that shapes our ends" had finally caught up with him. With the passage of years his son has "grown ever closer to the idea that Leslie's death was the final act of destiny at the moment his star was at zenith."

Howard himself had concluded his lectures on *Hamlet* with the "readiness is all" speech. "Not a whit, we defy augury. There's a special providence in the fall of a sparrow."

Still, the fact remains he had been knowingly sacrificed by his own people. Obviously Churchill knew better when, well after the war, he repeated the "mistaken identity" version of events. But then, Sir Winston was on record as against tampering with national myths. "The truth is so precious," he once declared. "That it must be protected with a bodyguard of lies."

It is this seemingly paradoxical notion of the truth being protected by a bodyguard of lies that brings us back to the question of not just "Who wrote Shakespeare?", but more importantly "Who cares? What does it matter?" It's a question well worth examining, because it leads to the idea that the truth being "protected" here is not some little thing, but something big, very big, and it matters a great deal. In this instance it matters so much that the truth of who Shakespeare really was had to be sacrificed.

In Shakespeare and Religion, G. Wilson Knight stated, "Probably the most important single suggestion in the following pages is that where I see Shakespeare's total work as, in structure, another Bible." This thought is not unique to Knight. Shakespeare has often been paired with the Bible and particularly with Jesus. If ever a new Messiah is to come, he will come, said Herman Melville, in the name of Shakespeare. "Jesus and Shakespeare are fragments of the soul, and by love I conquer and incorporate them in my own conscious domain," Emerson wrote in one of his essays. "When the gods come among men, they are not known. Jesus was not; Socrates and Shakespeare were not."

In fact both myths are touched with elements of the common and the miraculous. Both heros were of humble birth and rose through their native genius to overtop kings. Though little is known of their personal lives, in their work they celebrate the dignity and value of each individual human being. Jesus, king of kings, tells his followers that the kingdom of heaven is within. Emerson notes that "all that Shakespeare says of the king, yonder slip of a boy that reads in the corner feels to be true of himself."

This link between great and small is a large part of their meaning and their power. Yet how they achieved their triumphs is explained mainly in terms of the miraculous, at least to the faithful. Jesus was "the only begotten son of God" and Shakespeare possessed the "magic of genius," which is past understanding. Yet in the popular tradition they also represent a kind of mystery religion centered on the rise of a common man. Historically that kind of mythology has been very healthy for the development of Western, democratic institutions.

With this in mind the idea of accepting Shakespeare as a well-connected mortal could have provocative implications since the Prince who posed as Everyman is one way of interpreting the myth of Jesus himself.

One crisis of faith will lead to another. (In this regard it is interesting to note that Shakespeare never declared for the divinity of Christ. In fact he rarely mentions him by name and makes sure that in his own death/resurrection scenes it is very clear that the dramatic effect is being achieved through artifice.) Like other great works of art, the greatest. story ever told could be viewed as a fairytale that tells the truth, but a fairytale none the less. The political reverberations of such a revelation would be hard to underestimate. For the psychic appeal of this kind of hoax is very profound. W. H. Auden once observed that those "who write about Shakespeare reveal more about themselves than about Shakespeare, but perhaps that is [his] greatest value...whatever we may see taking place on stage, its final effect upon each spectator is self-revelation." In that mirror darkly, on the stage or that hill near Jerusalem, we each see ourselves. It may be there is a great fear of losing that in the collective unconscious of the Western mind. On the other hand there is nothing truer than truth, whatever form the messenger takes.

It was only a few generations before Shakespeare that Luther had unleashed the Reformation on Christendom. Luther's argument with the Pope had been theological but Henry VIII's had been political. He wanted to marry Anne Boylyn, Elizabeth's mother, but he also wanted the right to act independently of Rome whenever he wanted. By forming the Church of England he was essentially sanctifying the British Crown and investing it with the authority of a Pope.

It was this tumultuous, political, heretical world into which "Shakespeare" was born and in which he lived. And if the Oxfordian theory of the truth about Shakespeare is right, Shakespeare was not a spectator in this world, but rather a player who went on to leave his own mark upon this strange marriage of the Church of England and Christianity, a marriage that was solidified by a Virgin Queen Elizabeth (married only to her country) who oftentimes would publicly play the role of the Virgin Mary in religious ceremonies. And close to this mythic virgin was the man (Edward de Vere, 17th Earl of Oxford) who would become the greatest poet of his age, but never be known to have been that great poet. He was (and still is) erased from history.

In this 16th century retelling of the story, this erased/sacrificed author is resurrected, not as himself, but as "Shake-speare," a myth as entrancing and empowering as the original resurrection itself. And such myths cannot be exposed—it ruins the whole point of myths (remember the great line from the 1960 movie *The Man Who Shot Liberty Valance:* "When the legend becomes the fact, print the legend."). But where Christ had left behind merely disciples who told his story after his death, "Shake-speare" had written his own story in his own words. If myth-shattering truths (especially myths about the state and the church) were embedded in his writing, then he and his writing must be divorced from each other.

For some examples of the sort of "myth-shattering" truths that may be embedded in Shakespeare, let's take a look at two of his most famous plays, *Hamlet* and *King Lear.* In *Lear,* a play about a king and his three daughters, there is no mention of Queen Lear, no mention at all. This has been commented upon often in Shakespeare scholarship. There was even a play in the first part of a last century called *King Lear's Wife*[19] which attempted to answer this question of the missing queen.

In *Hamlet* we have a play which spends as much time on its secondary plot line (Polonius's family) as it does on Hamlet's problems with his uncle and his mother. In particular, what is the point of all the emphasis on Ophelia? What's with Hamlet and Ophelia? Is she, as some have speculated, pregnant? And if so, by whom?

Some 20th century scholars (e.g., Mark Taylor in *Shakespeare's Darker Purpose*, Marc Shell in *The End of Kinship*, and Janet Adelman in *Suffocating Mothers*) have looked at the problems in these two plays and made some interesting points about them. They have considered that the relationship between Lear and his daughters can explain both the missing Queen and the psychological complexities of the play. Lear is the husband as well as the father of all three daughters. And in *Hamlet* the issue of incest is not just about Gertrude and Claudius, but might be considered in the matter of how Ophelia got pregnant if not by Hamlet.

Some authors within the Oxfordian movement have considered this problem (Charlton Ogburn, Jr. and Mark Anderson) and pointed out that—if Ophelia is pregnant, and not by Hamlet—then the most likely suspect is her own father.[20] If such a thing could even be suspected 400 years ago, it is just one more reason that Robert Cecil would have had to be sure that the truth about the authorship (and thus the truth about which real life persons and events were being satirized) would be kept separate forever.

For those who have rejected the Stratford man as author, and have considered that only an insider with "intimate" knowledge of Elizabeth's court could be the true author, such theories about *King Lear* and *Hamlet* lead directly to major problems about truth, both historical and spiritual.

The Oxfordian movement has been grappling with these deeper, darker problems for decades, with some theorizing that not only was the real author Edward de Vere, 17th Earl of Oxford, but that in reality Edward de Vere may have been the first born of Queen Elizabeth in 1548 (at the time of her famous "rumored" pregnancy by Lord Admiral Thomas Seymour). And, further, that the two of them were also the parents of the third earl of Southampton, potentially the next king of England. All this is something our traditional, storybook Shakespeare can never do, let alone his monarch, the Virgin Queen. Think of Jesus and his mother. It's all just too much.[21]

So, enter the nobody author from Stratford. And so begins the conceit of imagination and genius explaining everything, nothing to see here, move along, move along.

Now let us think back to that dinner in 1940, the one with Clementine Churchill and all those prominent writers, and Leslie Howard , also a writer. Suppose at the end of the evening they talked about Edward de Vere as Shakespeare. Suppose that Howard at that dinner indicated that he just might put those "Oxford is Shakespeare" scenes in *Pimpernel Smith*. Most likely no one present said it was actually true, but almost certainly all said it should not be in a movie, not now at the beginning of a war for our very survival. But Howard might have said that's the way the Germans operate, i.e. suppressing the truth. And here we are, fighting so every person can be free to think his own thoughts. We must put forward the truth as we see it, not legends, he might have said. So that's all I'm doing. And what could any of them say to that? (This dinner gathering is dramatized in the screenplay in scene 43, on pages 123-126.)

Consider also that, although Leslie Howard had conversations with Winston Churchill concerning a movie about Lawrence of Arabia, had done great service during the war, had died by enemy gunfire, and had a dinner with Clementine Churchill in 1940—despite all this—Leslie Howard is not mentioned in three biographies about her.

What Howard may or may not have known about these particulars (changeling babies, bastard sons, incest) we cannot say. The theory about Southampton as the son of Oxford and Elizabeth had been published in pamphlets and newsletters in the 1930s, but not Oxford as the son of the Queen. Yet one feels he would have understood these ideas. And he would have been open to exploring all of them, and going where ever the trail might lead, no matter what. But what did the representatives of the state and the church think? More importantly, what did they know?

In any event, Leslie Howard, as a fledgling Oxfordian, was most likely coming to believe that the author of *Hamlet* had sacrificed not only his life but his very identity to the service of England, that there was indeed a special providence in the fall of a sparrow. And Leslie Howard, it is said, had a passion for England and the English ideal that was almost Shakespearean.

ENDNOTES:

1. After the war Laurence Olivier, a Stratfordian to the end, got a production of *Hamlet* to screen that was lacking in one interesting element—humor. Nevertheless it received an Academy award as Best Picture of 1948 and he won as Best Actor.

2. In Estel Eforgan's 2010 book *Leslie Howard: The Lost Actor* she says she could find no such headline in *Def Angriff*, or even any mention of Howard throughout the month of June 1943. The information about the headline comes from Ronald Howard's book about his father *(In Search of My Father)*, but we don't know where he got it, or whether or not it appeared somewhere other than *Der Angriff*.

3. This pattern of ignoring the fact of these scenes continues even today, as Eforgan also makes no mention of them. Perhaps no one talks about these scenes because there is no extant information about how and why Howard included them, or what anyone else thought about this decision. It should be noted here that records relating to Howard's estate that were supposed to have been declassified in 1980 were reclassified and will remain closed until Jan. 1, 2056. No one knows just what sort of records these are, let alone why they should remain classified until 113 years after Howard's death.

4. Twain, for example, said he could not be the man from Stratford, while Walt Whitman speculated that it had to be a nobleman. Herman Melville went even further. He had in ancestor who had traveled from Scotland to London with King James in 1603 (just after Queen Elizabeth's death), so perhaps he knew something. In Melville's last novel, the allegorical *Billy Budd* (published after both he and his wife were dead), he presents us with a captain, Edward Vere (nicknamed "Starry") who runs the ship from his reading room, and two key characters—Billy Budd and Claggert—who might then be seen as Henry Wriosthesley (Budd) and Robert Cecil (Claggert). A great injustice takes place, and in the end Billy Budd must be sacrificed (by hanging) in the name of "duty." He is a hanged man whose final words are, "God bless Captain Vere."

5. The word "pimpernel" appears only once in the official Shakespeare canon, in the curious "Induction Scene" that acts as a sort of curtain raiser to *The Taming of the Shrew*. During this scene an unnamed nobleman comes across a drunken lout lying in the middle of the road. As a jest he directs his servants to bathe and cloth this clown and place him in his own bed. When he awakens, all treat him as the Lord of the manor. The clown is astounded by the change in his circumstances, though none of it changes him. He soon falls asleep, bored and uncomprehending, as *The Shrew* is presented before him, and then disappears from the play.

"Pimpernel" is one of a list of names this commoner will forget ever having known since he has been reborn as a nobleman. Scholars have often pointed out that many actual Warwickshire residents appear on this list. In fact, this scene contains many of the most concrete references to Stratford and its environs that Shakespeare ever made.

6. In his book *Five and Eighty Hamlets* J.C. Trewin recalled seeing this production—"We know, alas, that little can be as dead as a stage biography of Shakespeare. *This Side Idolatry*, less embarrassing than most, included a Globe theater rehearsal of *Hamlet* that had judgement and reason on its side and illuminated a text otherwise shadowy. Though it expired after ten days, the last audience rose and cheered; when this happens there must be a cause that critics have not spied. It was not solely Howard's expertise and tact; his cast in general seemed to share a belief in the proceedings."

7. Minerva, the Roman goddess of wisdom, is drawn from a word that meant both "mind" and "man." It has a particular association for Oxfordians since Minerva in Greek mythology was Athena, the "hasti-vibrans" (spear-shaking) patron goddess of the Greek theater. In 1612 a London literary man named Henry Peacham published a book called *Minerva Britannia*. On its title page a proscenium arch setting is pictured with the curtain drawn back just enough to allow an arm with quill in hand to appear. The unseen writer has just penned in Latin the words MENTE.VIDE BORI — "By the mind shall I be seen." These letters form a perfect anagram for the phrase TIBI NOM. DE VERE — "Thy name. De Vere."

8. "According to a story by the Southeast Missourian newspaper, Howard could be a difficult man to track down, wandering off the set between takes. One day Tay Garnett, while directing *Stand-In* (1937), had to have several men take him into custody. With the gentleness due a star, they tied him up, clapping leg irons on him. Garnett finally put him on probation, but gave Howard a cowbell and ordered him to bong the bell when on a stroll. It wasn't long before a scene was ready for shooting --- but no Howard. Soon enough they heard the cowbell, though, in a distant corner of the sound stage and up in the catwalks. Converging in on the sound, they found only the bell with a string attached. They traced the string over rafters back to the lighted set where *Stand-In* was suppose to be shooting. There sat Mr. Howard, yanking at the string, plaintively indignant about the absence of Director Garnett." (From the Imbd biography of Howard.)

What they didn't realize was that Howard hated this film—a second rate comedy with a bad ending—and wished he were not there. It was the last of a three picture deal with Warner Bros. That's why he did what he did—it was his form of a protest. From this point forward he would only deal with one picture at a time.

9. Rex Harrison played Higgins on Broadway and in the 1964 motion picture. Harrison once quipped to writer Earl Wilson, "Actually, my dear fellow, I play Leslie [Howard] doing Higgins" (from the Wikipedia article on Howard; they do not provide a citation for it).

10. Margaret Mitchell described Howard as "every Southerner's first choice to play Ashley" and Selznick too quickly realized that only an actor with his innate intelligence and truly aristocratic bearing could counter the appeal of Gable's extraordinary magnetism. Without that balance Scarlet's indecision in choosing between them would look foolish and implausible to the audience. His presence was essential to the film's success, and Selznick went to great lengths to get Howard.

Howard's fate forms a striking contrast to the wartime experience of his *Gone with the Wind* co-star. Like Howard, Clark Gable lost the love of his life when Carole Lombard was killed in the other famous movie star air crash of World War II. Devastated by the loss and haunted by the sense that movie acting was a trivial pursuit in such times, he enlisted in the Army Air Corps, telling a friend he didn't much care if he returned or not. He was sent to England as a gunner in B-17's. But, in truth, the Air Corps didn't really know what to do with its glamorous, humble and over-age recruit. He begged for combat missions and flew with a few but Hitler had reportedly offered a reward to the pilot who shot the King, his favorite star, out of the sky. This distinction probably did not make him the most sought after of crew-mates. For whatever reasons he ended up being used in a routine string of publicity and training films. Crushed and humiliated, he mustered out before war's end.

So Gable lived and resumed his career as the screen's most self-assured winner. But then Howard had always played the self-sacrificing hero as if to the manner born. He would have made an interesting Victor Laszlo in *Casablanca*—he was, after all, a Jew from Hungary—had he not already been booked on his own Lisbon flight.

11. It is an interesting coincidence that Stacpoole's middle name is de Vere, and that the subject of his book is mistaken identity

involving an English earl and a commoner. The book had been made into a silent film in 1920. The war interfered with Howard's plan, yet another film based on the book did come out in 1941, produced by Universal Pictures in Hollywood.

12. This story is cited from Eforgan (163). Her source can be found on page 238 of Nigel Nicolson's *Harold Nicolson: Diaries and Letters 1907-1964* (cited in Eforgan 169, fn 48).

13. "In England," Howard once said, "Acting is an honorable profession. A gentleman's job as well as a man's job. The type of Englishman who takes up acting as his life's work is most often like the kind of American chap who goes in for banking or the law."

Though born into a family of bankers Raoul Wallenberg would have made, according to his sister, "a great actor. He could imitate brilliantly. If he wanted to, he could be more German than a Prussian general." Though normally his manner was subdued and his voice soft, he is credited with saving a thousand Jews from the Nazis in Hungary. He did this while acting as a special envoy to the Swedish delegation stationed in Budapest during the winter of 1944, passing out thousands of passports, setting up dozens of "safe" houses, and facing down Adolf Eichmann and other murderers with nothing more than diplomatic immunity for protection.

"Raoul just wasn't a political person," his sister would later recall. "He did what he did out of his feelings. He hated stupid bullies and pompous people and he hated seeing people pushed around."

After the Russians finally occupied Budapest Raoul was taken east to the Hungarian city of Debrecen. And there he disappeared, probably into the Gulag, forever. Apparently the Russians could not believe he wasn't a spy.

Russian sources claim he died not long after the war but there are those who believe he is still alive somewhere. Reported sightings keep cropping up, one in a Soviet prison for those who are supposed to be officially dead.

Right after the war the people of Budapest tried to honor him. A huge statue of St. George slaying the dragon was to symbolize his struggle against the Nazis. It was to be unveiled on a Sunday afternoon in April, 1948. But the night before soldiers came and carted the memorial away. All that remained was the pedestal.

Recently, in the city where Rauol Wallenberg disappeared the monument to him reappeared—but without his name.

14. Anthony Eden's letter to Leslie Howard, dated 20 April 1943, is quoted (219) in Estel Eforgan's *Leslie Howard: The Lost Actor* (2010). Eforgan introduces the letter by saying that, "But Eden was determined. He replied to Leslie's fears rather lightly."

> I can quite understand your scruples about hobnobbing with Falangist leaders in Spain, but I do not think they need worry you unduly, or affect your plans for the journey. The Falangists although tiresome and influential are only a minority in Spain, and it is, I think, unlikely that you will come into contact with many friends there, who are to be found in all classes. On the whole I think it would be best to avoid Spanish internal politics as a subject of conversation, and to concentrate on explaining the British war effort. First hand reports on this subject are of special value in a country like Spain, where the Axis have succeeded in reducing our publicity to a minimum...
>
> I do not think either that you need fear that your journey will be misinterpreted by the Russians, who take a realistic view of Spanish affairs and of the importance of Spanish neutrality to the United Nations war effort.

15. There is no mention in Eden's memoirs nor in his biography by Robert Rhodes James of this dinner, nor of any of his dealings with Leslie Howard and his trip to Spain. The name "Leslie Howard" does not appear in the index of either book.

16. From Charlton Ogburn's *The Mysterious William Shakespeare*, p. 162.

17. Other passengers were bumped from this flight (to accommodate Howard and Chenhalls), among them, " ... the teenage sons of Cornelia Stuyvesant Vanderbilt: George and William Cecil, who had been recalled to London from their Swiss boarding school. Being bumped by Howard saved their lives. William Cecil is best associated with his ownership and preservation of his grandfather George Washington Vanderbilt's Biltmore estate in North Carolina. William Cecil described a story after several months back in London in which he met a woman who said she had secret war information and used his mother's phone to put in a call to the British Air

Ministry. She told them that she had a message from Leslie Howard."(From the Wikipedia entry for Leslie Howard)

From the point of view of this essay it can only be ironic that two Cecils (William and George) were spared by the killing of Leslie Howard, just as one of an earlier generation of Cecils (i,e., Robert Cecil) saved his political career (and maybe his life) by sacrificing—politically—Edward de Vere.

18. Stevenson's book and this quote are not mentioned in Eforgan's book. However, on the very last page (245), following all the footnotes, she does reproduce a letter from Mavis Batey (a decoder at Bletchley Park in WWII), to whom she had apparently written in 2002 asking about whether British Intelligence would have let the civilian airliner with Howard onboard go down in order to protect their decoding breakthrough. Batey says in her letter that if such a message had been decoded, "it was not ignored to save Enigma." Batey cites other examples in her letter of how decoded information could be acted upon without tipping off the Germans that their code had been broken. Eforgan does not mention Batey's letter in her final chapter, and does not address directly this matter of whether or not British Intelligence did have foreknowledge of the German attack and failed to act on it.

19. Bottomley, Gordon. *King Lear's Wife and Other Plays* (Boston, Small, Maynard and Co., 1915).

20. Mark Anderson's essay "Ophelia's Difference" (*Shakespeare Oxford Newsletter*, Winter 2000) on Ophelia's "problem" is not the only one to posit that she is pregnant, but once one goes down that road the question then becomes "pregnant by whom?" The case that Anderson makes for her father Polonius as the culprit is persuasive and stunning. Charlton Ogburn, in his *The Mysterious William Shakespeare*, also considers this scenario (page 575) in his discussion of how Anne Cecil (the model for Ophelia) may have gotten pregnant if it wasn't by her husband, Edward de Vere.

21. An alternate view of the history of Jesus has been told in such popular books as *The Passover Plot* and *Holy Blood, Holy Grail*. Simply summed up, this alternate view is that there was no virgin birth at the beginning nor an actual death and resurrection at the end.

Instead there were "stories," climaxing in one of the grandest "performances" of the ages (the crucifixation and resurrection), all part of the Greatest Story Ever Told. Furthermore, whether the universe really is divine and all the people in it eternal is not the point here. What is important is consideration that a difference is being drawn between the belief in the "divinity" of Jesus (Son of God) and the ministry of Jesus (The Teacher). Some believe that the divinity gets in the way of understanding the ministry, while others are equally convinced that the divinity of Jesus is what matters most. I suppose the only way to resolve this is to declare all people divine—whether they know it or not.

ANOTHER HAMLET:

THE MYSTERY OF LESLIE HOWARD

An original screenplay

by

Charles Boyle

(©1995, 2011, 2013)

Setting:

Action takes place in New York, London, Hollywood, Lisbon, Madrid and Berlin (and local environs of each) from 1935 to 1943.

Cast:

Leslie Howard	English actor
Ruth Howard	His wife
Doodie Howard	His daughter
Wink Howard	His son
Merle Oberon	English-Indian actress
Violette Cunningham	English-French actress
John Geilgud	English actor
Vivian Leigh	English actress
David Niven	English actor
Mary Morris	English actress
Humphrey Bogart	American actor
Gabriel Pascal	Film producer
Alfred Chenhalls	Film producer
John Houseman	Film producer/director
Schuyler Watts	A graduate student
Winston Churchill	Prime Minister of England
Anthony Eden	Secretary of Foreign Affairs
Jack Beddington	British Council
Dr. Walter Starkie	British official
Joseph Goebbels	Propaganda Minister, Germany
Baroness von Podewils	Wife of Count von Podewils, a German citizen

Scene 1 - Prologue

A close up of Bette Davis on screen delivering this tirade into camera.

"Yew cad, yew dirty swine. I never cared for yew – not once. Yew always made a fool of yuh. It made me sick when yew had to let me kiss me. I only did it because you begged me. Yew hounded me, it drove me crazy, and, after yew kissed me, I'll always used to wipe my mouth...wipe my mouth."

ANGLE ON JOSEPH GOEBBELS, NAZI MINISTRY OF PROPAGANDA
In his own private screening room sit in next to his wife, who is knitting, he watches the screen with utter fascination. His wife glances at him furtively.

ANGLE ON SCREEN
Leslie Howard's face - is sensitive, intelligent eyes filled with pain.

DAVIS
"For every kiss I had to laugh. We laughed at you because you're such a mug, a mug, a monster. You're a cripple, a cripple, a cripple."

ANGLE ON GOEBBELS' WIFE
She is visibly uncomfortable, glancing at him while he stares at screen, his eyes brimming. We see him rise and LIMP to the bar to pour a drink.

Scene 2 - New York, 1935

EXT. NEW YORK CITY - DAY - ESTABLISHING
a street in the theater district

ANGLE ON A MARQUEE, HUGE LETTERS
"Leslie Howard in The Petrified Forest"
in smaller letters, "Opening Friday!"

42

ANGLE ON PUBLICITY PHOTOS
of Howard in stark confrontation with Humphrey Bogart.

ANGLE ON
LESLIE HOWARD, a slender, mysterious and poeticly handsome
man, of uncanny grace and quickness, dressed in a large overcoat
and broad brimmed hat, pushes open the lobby door.

ANGLE ON HOWARD'S FACE
as he glances about him with eyes full of pain and desire, pulls
down his hat, and slips away silently as a ghost.

EXT. NEW YORK AIRPORT - AFTERNOON - ESTABLISHING

ANGLE ON HOWARD
as he skirts past a reporter to board a DC-3 airliner.

EXT. DC-3 - NIGHT - ESTABLISHING
as it flies through an intense electrical storm.

INT. DC-3 - NIGHT - MED. SHOT
as Howard puts down newspaper with large photo of Hitler, huge
Nazi flag in background, harranging a crowd. Howard sighs
heavily and looks out porthole.

HOWARD'S POV
surly clouds like a war torn landscape illuminated by lightening,
the illusion lashing like a dream of the gathering storm.

TITLES ROLL

Scene 3 - Hollywood, 1935

EXT. HOLLYWOOD AIRPORT - MORNING - ESTABLISHING
plane landing in beautiful sunshine, a discreet and eager Howard
walks quickly along.

EXT. BEAUTIFUL HOLLYWOOD HOME - DAY
Howard, his coat over his arm, strides up to the front door.

INT. HALLWAY - DAY
as the incredibly beautiful MERLE OBERON opens the door and
Howard rushes into her embrace.

HOWARD
We open tomorrow night, I'll have to fly back in the
morning. (She kisses him.)

INT. BEDROOM - NIGHT
Soft MUSIC playing. Slow pan of elegant mess - remains of
champagne and caviar on a silver tray, candles burned down and
sputtering, her silk robe with ostrich trim and French lingerie
scattered with his jacket and trousers on a thick white carpet - the
whole scene reminiscent of a luxurious romance movie of that
era. Camera pans up slowly to find them lying amidst the silk
sheets and satin quilts. She is running her finger along the
delicate, aristocratic line of his nose.

HOWARD
I can't bear being without you.

OBERON
We could begin a new life together.

HOWARD
I know.

EXT. NIGHT - DREAM SEQUENCE
A First World War battlefield that looks like the landscape of
clouds he saw in flight. Darkness, swirling mist, flashes like
lightening, booming sounds like THUNDER growing ever closer
till the earth seems to be erupting. Men all around are
SCREAMING, some cry for their mothers, till all are overwhelmed
by the oncoming barrage. We SEE Howard observing it all from a
nearby hill.

INT. HALLWAY - NIGHT
as Howard crashes through doorway, YELLING incoherently.

INT. BEDROOM - NIGHT

Oberon awakened by the commotion. She looks around, he isn't there. She rushes to find him still crashing through the house, slamming doors and turning on lights.

OBERON
Leslie! Leslie, darling! What is it? (She shakes him awake) Leslie, what's wrong?

HOWARD
(After he has calmed down, still breathing heavily) I'm sorry. It's alright. Just one of my bad dreams.

OBERON
I've never seen you like this before. What dreams?

HOWARD
Battles, mainly, strange battles... had them ever since the war...

OBERON
Oh, darling...

HOWARD

(Pauses) I thought why walk when you can ride? So I joined the Cavalry. Somehow we all thought it was going to be an old fashioned war, full of plumes and glory. Well, it was hell on earth, and all for nothing. The fact is I came back in a very bad way. I returned togEand numb to the world. (Pauses) Merle, come to New York, please. I'll leave Ruth.(They look at each other and hug. He looks over her shoulder into space, afraid).

EXT. HOLLYWOOD AIRPORT - DAY - MED. SHOT
Oberon and Howard standing by the gate, DC-3 in B.G.

OBERON
Good luck, darling,. I wish I could be there. Break a leg.

HOWARD
I'll be thinking of you.

OBERON
How is that new actor working out?

HOWARD
Bogart? He certainly makes a convincing stand-in for
Hitler.

Scene 4 - New York, 1935

CUT TO:
INT. THEATER - NIGHT
CLOSE-UP OF BOGART
unshaven and mean-eyed, other ACTORS playing gangsters in b.g.
on the desert cafe set of The Petrified Forest.

BOGART
Just keep in mind that me and the boys are candidates for
hanging, and the minute anybody makes the wrong move,
I'm going to kill the whole lot of you. (He looks at
Howard) So keep your seats. (Silence as he continues his
hard, empty stare)

REACTION SHOT
of Howard in play, in character, listening thoughtfully.

ANGLE ON
a distinguished and entranced opening night audience. Amidst the
glitter and glamor we SEE three figures sitting together, down
front center, who are clearly Howard's family. RUTH HOWARD,
a plain, once handsome matron, WINK, a boy of seventeen, and
DOODIE, a girl of twelve, who watches her father with awe.

ANGLE ON HOWARD
there is a luminous clarity to his acting.

HOWARD
You see, the trouble with me is, I belong to a vanishing

race. I'm one of the intellectuals, brains without purpose. Noise without sound. Shadow without substance...we thought we'd conquered Nature. But this chaos is nature hitting back...she's deliberately afflicting mankind with the jitters. She's taking the world away from the intellectuals and giving it back to the apes. (Smiles at Bogart and adds with subtle irony) But this document will be my ticket to immortality. It will inspire people to say: 'There was an artist, who died before his time!' (Pause) Will you do it, Duke?

                    BOGART
(Cruel and flat) I'll be glad to.

SLOW PAN
of audience sitting in absolute stillness.

DISSOLVE TO FINAL SCENE
on stage ACTORS playing hostages are being hustled out the cafe set door.

                    ACTORS
Don't shoot - don't shoot. For god's sakes, buddies, don't shoot!

ANGLE ON BOGART
in doorway, a crouched silhouette against the theatrical moonlit, a machine gun under his arm, a revolver in his hand. Howard and the ACTRESS playing his love interest are hiding under a table.

                    BOGART
You'd better stay where you are. Good night, folks.

                    HOWARD
(Springing to his feet) Duke!

                    ACTRESS
Alan! Keep down!

HOWARD

Duke!

BOGART

Do you still want it?

HOWARD

(Desperately) It's no matter whether I want it or not.
You've got to ...

BOGART

Okay, pal. (He SHOOTS the revolver at Howard, who
spins against the lunch counter. The actress SCREAMS)

ANGLE ON DOODIE
crying, the audience around her stunned and silent.

DISSOLVE TO CURTAIN CALLS
*rising applause and whistles as Bogart takes his bow. When
Howard appears the crowd jumps to their feet, cheering. Smiling,
he grasps Bogart's hand, holds it aloft, and they bow together.*

INT. BOGART'S DRESSING ROOM - NIGHT
Howard is standing in the doorway, about to leave.

BOGART

(Very grateful, almost obsequious) Thanks again, Leslie.
None of this would have happened without you.

HOWARD

It's my pleasure. It's one of the pleasures of being a
producer.

BOGART

Thanks for believing in me.

HOWARD

I just saw what you already have.

EXT. STAGE DOOR - NIGHT - FULL SHOT
Howard, guarded by two STAGEHANDS, is mobbed by a horde of
adoring female FANS as he steps out the door. He is pulled away
by two beautiful YOUNG WOMEN in evening gowns who tear at
his clothing and his hair, one with small nail scissors. He jumps
away, only to be seized by another lovely DEBUTANTE, who
kisses him. All around him young women are pawing and calling
out impassioned pleas of everlasting devotion. Some are crying.
An orgiastic fervor pervades the scene.

ANGLE ON A THIRD STORY WINDOW
as a grinning Bogart watches from his dressing room.

BOGART'S POV
as Howard's blonde head, bobbing amid the swirling sea of
females, is pulled to safety in the waiting limo.

Scene 5 - New York, 1935 (same night)

INT. LIMO'S BACKSEAT - NIGHT
where his family awaits. Ruth eyes him skeptically.

> HOWARD
> I used to watch Katharine Cornell battling through a
> frightful mob like that every night. My goodness, I
> thought, wouldn't it be exciting to be so famous - but you
> know, it isn't so pleasant after all.

> WINK
> (With mock concern) All those screaming women.

> HOWARD
> Yes, it's positively pagan.

Scene 6 - New York, 1935

INT. HOWARD'S BEDROOM - NIGHT - RUTH'S FACE
her eyes full of tears.

RUTH

Ever since your first success I've watched them come after you, these hardboiled, emancipated women, proclaiming their disgust with everything our mothers held dear. A baby's a "mistake" and a husband just part of a stamp collection to be traded around. And I used to be afraid of them, used to think they were sophisticated, the way they drank like men and smoked like men and carried on like men and still they thought they weren't whores.

HOWARD

You didn't seem so afraid.

RUTH

I've always been afraid. (Cries)

HOWARD

(Coming to her) Darling, you know I love you. Nothing can take the place of you and the children. In the end I'm the fellow who creeps home and puts his head in his best girl's lap.

INT. OBERON'S BEDROOM - NIGHT
Oberon is on the phone.

OBERON

Have you told her?

INT. HOWARD'S HOTEL ROOM - NIGHT

HOWARD

Oh, she knows, but I haven't asked for a divorce yet. Not right now, in the middle of a Broadway run. I have a responsibility to the rest of the cast. After all I am one of the producers and there's no telling how this disruption to my 'perfect family image' will go down with the public. Then there's the question of the children...

INTERCUT

> OBERON
> We both have public lives, I know...

> HOWARD
> (Whispering softly) I'll make reservations at a hotel near here. (He turns to SEE Doodie in the doorway. His tone becomes business-like) But right now I'm in rehearsals with my new leading lady for an appearance on Rudy Vallee's radio show.

> OBERON
> New leading lady?

> HOWARD
> My absolute favorite. Doodie!

ANGLE ON DOODIE
smiling up at him.

> HOWARD
> We're doing a scene in which a man who longs for a daughter finds her on Mid-Summer's Eve, only to discover she is just a shade, a figment of his longing, a might-have-been...

> OBERON
> Sounds charming.

> HOWARD
> I'm glad it's only a play. (Leans down to Doodie) Honey, could you find Daddy's pipe? I think it's in the bedroom. (She runs off. Softly to Oberon) I love you.

ANGLE ON DOODIE
watching wonderingly from door.

EXT. DC-3 IN FLIGHT - DAY - ESTABLISHING
INT. DC-3 - DAY
Oberon looks out the porthole, smiling.

OBERON'S POV
of fairy castle clouds hanging in a brilliant sky.

Scene 7 - New York, 1935

INT. HOWARD'S LIVING ROOM - EVENING
Doodie is rehearsing the scene with him.

> HOWARD
> Now relax and repeat after me. (Reading line) <u>Don't</u> go into that house, Daddy - I don't know <u>why</u> it is, but I'm <u>afraid</u> of that house.

> DOODIE
> (Mimicking him perfectly) <u>Don't</u> go into that house, Daddy. I don't know <u>why</u> it is, but I'm <u>afraid</u> of that house.

> HOWARD
> Very good! You made me believe it. (Doodie smiles up at him)

INT. APARTMENT BEDROOM - NIGHT - DOODIE
in bed, listening to her father whispering in the other room, we
HEAR her work herself into a fit of tears.

> DOODIE
> Daddy! Daddy!

ANGLE ON HOWARD
rushing in.

> HOWARD
> Darling, darling, what is it?

> DOODIE
> I don't want to be a might-have-been either, Daddy!

> HOWARD
> You're not, my darling - there, there. You'll never be a might-have-been. (He soothes her to sleep, stroking her

face and whistling softly his own special tune. Then he
stares into the dark, worried)

INT. SUMPTUOUS HOTEL ROOM - EVENING
as Howard sweeps in with Oberon.

> HOWARD
> I've taken a room above. We must be discreet.

> OBERON
> I know.

> HOWARD
> I hate all this deception. (They tumble towards the bed)

Scene 8 - New York, 1935

INT. NEW YORK THEATER - DAY
Howard is being interviewed by an audience of STUDENTS. Ruth
is in the front row.

> STUDENT ONE
> What do you think of autograph hunters?

> HOWARD
> Bad manners. They belong to the movies and the typical
> movie fan is a freak. (Students laugh)

> STUDENT TWO
> Do you expect to always be an actor or to go one to
> something better? (Nervous laughter from students)

> HOWARD
> (Gravely) Hmmm. I've always wanted to better myself in
> life. I will leave when I can do something equally well or
> better. I've written plays and I want to produce and direct
> films.

ANGLE ON SCHUYLER WATTS
a sharp young graduate student

                    WATTS
        Do you want to play Hamlet?

                    HOWARD
        Every actor wants to play Hamlet.

INT. THEATER LOBBY - DAY
Watts, a script in hand, walks up to Howard and Ruth.
                    WATTS
   Mr. Howard?

                    HOWARD
   Yes?

                    WATTS
   My name is Schuyler Watts. I've seen you in *Petrified*
   Forest. Thought you were excellent.

                    HOWARD
   Thank you.

                    WATTS
   You should play Hamlet.

CLOSE-UP
of Howard, his eyes lighting.

                    WATTS
   While I was at Yale I became fascinated with Hamlet. I
   have a version I'd like you to read. (Hands him the script)

                    HOWARD
   Why should I play Hamlet?

                    WATTS
   Well, you must be tired of always playing yourself.

ANGLE ON RUTH
taken aback.

HOWARD

Hmmm. (He nods and smiles thoughtfully) A few seasons ago I played William Shakespeare in London... (he thinks for a moment) ... I'd be glad to look at this. Come round the theater next week and we'll talk.

RUTH

(As Watts leaves) What a strange young man!

Scene 9 - New York, 1935

INT. HOTEL ROOM - LATE MORNING
Oberon is reading aloud from a newspaper to Howard.

OBERON

...we do wonder why Mr. Howard has never bothered to enlarge his field, to play the truly courageous part in the theater which could so easily be his.

HOWARD

Yes...?

OBERON

...it leaves one wondering why a man who ought to make an interesting Hamlet... (She stops)

HOWARD

Yes. (Takes paper from her) ...should have elected to be so unadventurous as an actor." (Pause) Well, next season I plan to play Hamlet...and then we'll see. Critics!

OBERON

Next season...

HOWARD

Perhaps you could play Ophelia.

OBERON

Perhaps Ruth could play Gertrude.

HOWARD

Darling, once this show closes I'll tell her. Soon you'll be starring in films I make. And they'll be great films.

OBERON

And there never was a producer so beautiful... (They kiss)

INSERT HOTEL ROOM DOOR - TIGHT SHOT
as a youthful hand knocks on it.

BACK TO SCENE
Howard and Oberon break apart. Oberon instinctively exits to the bedroom. Howard crosses to the door and opens it. We SEE Wink standing there, smiling.

HOWARD

Wink!

WINK

Hi, Dad.

HOWARD

What are you doing here at this hour?

WINK

Mother wanted me to remind you that you promised Doodie you'd take her riding in Central Park this morning.

HOWARD

Yes, yes, of course.

WINK

You forgot last time.

HOWARD

Of course, I remember.

WINK

Shall I wait for you?

                    HOWARD
        Hmmm....

ANGLE ON OBERON
fully dressed, coming from the bedroom.

                    OBERON
        Good morning, Ronald.

ANGLE ON WINK
as his eyes go wide.

                    WINK
        Good morning.

                    HOWARD
        Wink, this is Merle Oberon.

                    WINK
        How do you do.

                    OBERON
        It's a pleasure to meet you. You look a lot like your
        father.

                    WINK
        Thank you. (An awkward silence. Oberon looks at
        Howard)

                    HOWARD
        Ronald, Merle is going to be your new step-mother.

CLOSE-UP
of Wink's amazed reaction.

CHANGE LOCATION - CLOSE-UP
of Wink's face as he recounts the story.

                    WINK
        ...and then he said, "This is your new step-mother."

ANGLE ON RUTH
her face full of shock and anger. Doodie quiet in b.g.

Scene 10 - New York, 1935

INT. HOTEL ROOM - NIGHT
Oberon is sitting with a distraught Howard.

> HOWARD
> Ruth's taken the children to California. She's going to file
> for a divorce.

> OBERON
> Wouldn't Reno have been quicker?

> HOWARD
> We have friends in California.

> OBERON
> Well, at least now it's out. Soon it'll be over.

> HOWARD
> I know...I miss the children.

> OBERON
> You'll still see them.

> HOWARD
> I know...but it won't be the same...God, I'm tired! I'm so
> sick of this show. (She puts her hand to his forehead)

> OBERON
> Darling, you're burning up. You've got a fever. You've got
> to rest.

INT. BEDROOM - EVENING - CLOSE-UP
of Howard 's nose with a large boil on it.

CAMERA PULLS BACK
to reveal Howard in bed, with a terrible case of boils all over his

body. Oberon is standing by him.

> OBERON
> Feeling any better?

> HOWARD
> Dreadful.

> OBERON
> Oh, poor baby. *The Scarlet Pimpernel* opens tomorrow
> night.

> HOWARD
> I've got scarlet pimpernels opening all over my body.
> Besides, I'll be doing the play...

> OBERON
> Oh, darling...rest.

> HOWARD
> (Firmly) I'll be doing the play.

Scene 11 - New York, 1935

INT. MOVIE THEATER - NIGHT
ANGLE ON SCREEN
newsreel of JOSEPH GOEBBELS, the Nazi Minister of
Propaganda, making a speech. His words are subtitled.

> GOEBBELS
> There can be no propaganda without the nation and no
> nation without good propaganda! And if the Jewish press
> would attempt to deny Germany's great destiny, I say to
> the mighty Jewish press, beware, how the mighty have
> fallen.

NEWSREEL SCENES
of book burnings.

REACTION SHOT OF OBERON

sitting among distinguished opening night audience, disturbed by these scenes.

ANGLE ON SCREEN - MONTAGE
of scenes from The Scarlet Pimpernel*," beginning with titles, Howard's name large and Oberon's small. Then a scene of a guillotine falling, a daring escape on a wagon driven by an old crone and then the crone peeling off her disguise to reveal Howard beneath. Next we SEE Howard being an ineffectual fop with Oberon, reciting his little ditty.*

> HOWARD (In movie)
> They see him here, they see him there
> Those Frenchies see him everywhere
> Is he in Heaven? Is he in Hell?
> Where is that Scarlet Pimpernel?

Then we SEE him rescuing her from the villain and escaping onto a sailship.

CLOSE-UP OF HOWARD

> HOWARD (In movie)
> This royal throne of kings, this scept'red isle,
> This earth of majesty, this seat of Mars...
> This happy breed of men, this little world,
> This precious stone set in the silver sea...
> This blessed plot, this earth, this realm, this England!

ANGLE ON
Howard and Oberon together on the ship.

> OBERON (In movie)
> Look! England!

We SEE in the movie the cliffs of Dover through the fog. "The End." APPLAUSE O.S.

ANGLE ON AUDIENCE
we SEE Oberon being congratulated by various people.

INT. BEDROOM - LATER THAT NIGHT
Oberon sits down on Howard's bed.

> OBERON
>
> Oh, I wish you could have been there! Everyone loved it, loved the Shakespeare at the end.

> HOWARD
>
> Did they draw any parallels with the current situation and Mister Hitler?

> OBERON
>
> Oh, nobody wants to think about that. There was a newsreel of them burning books and that horrible Goebbels man blaming the Jews for everything.

> HOWARD
>
> Didn't mention me, did he?

> OBERON
>
> Nobody knows you're a Jew.

> HOWARD
>
> But did anyone get the point? Someday England may have to fight these crazy Nazis, just like we did Napoleon and the Reign of Terror.

> OBERON
>
> Leslie, these are Americans, they don't care. But they love you. (She starts to kiss him, he winces) Baby, you should rest. Let your understudy do the show.

> HOWARD
>
> \   No, I can do it.

> OBERON
>
> Baby, the doctor says there's a blood vein near that one that leads straight to the brain.

HOWARD
I know, I know. Don't worry. I can do the show. That's what people are paying to see.

OBERON
Oh, stop being the producer for one minute...

HOWARD
(Snapping) Just let me rest, will you! (Pause) Darling, I'm sorry. But you know you can't be seen constantly in my suite. These gossip columnists will bribe maids for a story.

OBERON
(Softly, firmly) Leslie, what are you saying?

HOWARD
Ruth called last night...she's returning to New York with the children. I thought I could break away...but this illness has convinced me...I can't break up my family...I thought I could...but...

ANGLE ON OBERON
she is stunned.

HOWARD (O.S.)
...my wife and children are essential to my existence.

INT. BEDROOM - MORNING
Howard is propped up in bed, surrounded by his family.

RUTH
Leslie, you look like hell. (They all laugh together, he places his head against Ruth's bosom)

HOWARD
Lets close this show and return home to England!

Scene 12 - Stowe Maries (Howard's home), England, 1935

MONTAGE (footage from Howard's recently rediscovered home

movies can be use here) Howard and family sailing for England, then settling in at Stowe Maries, their Tudor home in Surrey. We SEE him playing the country squire, riding horses with Doodie, taking tea. We HEAR the phone ring. Howard picks it up.

INT. DRAB HOLLYWOOD APARTMENT - DAY
Bogart is on the telephone.

> BOGART
> (Anxious) Hello, Leslie?

INTERCUT

> HOWARD
> Bogie! Can you afford this call?

> BOGART
> Listen. I just heard Warners is giving my part to Edward G. Robinson. 'They don't need another gangster.'

> HOWARD
> They need me. (And they won't get me without you.z)

Scene 13 - Hollywood, filming *Petrified Forest*, 1935

INT. HOLLYWOOD MOVIE SET - DAY
the cafe set of The Petrified Forest.

ANGLE ON ACTOR
standing by the door.

> ACTOR
> This is Duke Mantee, folks. He's the world-famous killer and he's hungry.

CLOSE-UP OF BOGART
as he steps thru the door the DIRECTOR yells "Cut!"

> DIRECTOR
> Very nice, very nice. Everyone relax while we fix the

lights.

TWO SHOT
Bogart and Howard

BOGART
So Shakespeare, how's Hamlet coming?

HOWARD
Everything seems to be falling into place. In fact, I've just
been offered Romeo opposite Norma Shearer in a movie
version.

BOGART
Romeo?

HOWARD
You think I'm a little long in the tooth for Romeo?
(Bogart laughs) It was first offered to Gielgud, but he
turned it down. Doesn't think Shakespeare should be
filmed. (Bogart laughs again)

BOGART
He may be right.

HOWARD
Maybe it's a baby Hamlet. Got to start somewhere.

ANGLE ON SCRIPT GIRL
as she approaches Howard, obviously smitten

SCRIPT GIRL
Oh, Mr. Howard, I've got those *Hamlet* revisions you
asked me to type.

HOWARD
Oh, yes, yes. (Looks about, vaguely distracted) I'll tell
you what. Let's find some place where we can go over
these together. (Glancing at Bogart) Excuse us, old boy.

BOGART

(Grinning broadly) Don't worry, Leslie, I was wrong, you'll be a very believable Romeo.

Scene 14 - Hollywood, filming *Romeo and Juliet*, 1936

INT. CLOSE-UP OF HOWARD
looking very healthy and radiant in a full Elizabethan costume

HOWARD

Readiness is all, gentlemen...

CAMERA PULLS BACK
to reveal him in what appears to be an Elizabethan setting.
Howard is conferring with JOHN HOUSEMAN, his co-director,
and Watts on the set of Romeo and Juliet

HOWARD

The sets, the costumes, everything will be done in the authentic style of 11th century Denmark. We'll spare no expense. First class, all the way.

HOUSEMAN

You're the producer. I can tell you word of this coming *Hamlet* is already arousing great anticipation in New York.

HOWARD

Yes, this is my bid to 'prove' myself. Even the British think I'm only an American actor.

HOUSEMAN

Well, they all want to play Hamlet. Why not you?

WATTS

You know, I always think of Hamlet as Shakespeare himself. It must be a self-portrait.

HOWARD

Yes, a theater man. The only time he's ever truly happy

and himself is when he's with the players. It's like he's one of them.

WATTS

But look at the rest. He had the soul of an artist, but circumstances thrust him onto an infinitely more dangerous political stage. That was his tragedy.

HOUSEMAN

Whose?

WATTS

Well, Hamlet's.

HOUSEMAN

Oh, for a minute there I thought you meant Shakespeare.

WATTS

Perhaps him too. If he even was Shakespeare.

HOUSEMAN

(Sharply) What's that supposed to mean?

WATTS

We know so little about him. I mean, we can all agree he was an artist but he writes so well about politics it makes you wonder if he wasn't there.

HOUSEMAN

You're not starting this Shakespeare wasn't Shakespeare rubbish, are you?

WATTS

It's a question that's been in the air a hundred years now.

HOUSEMAN

In the air is right. Stinking up the place.

WATTS

Being a bit stiff necked, aren't we?

HOWARD

Gentlemen, gentlemen, let's not come to blows. It's a fine mystery and I tremble every day least something should turn up.

Scene 15 - New York/Boston, rehearsing *Hamlet*, 1936

INT. REHEARSAL HALL NEW YORK
camera pans slowly across the faces of eight beautiful women

ANGLE ON HOUSEMAN

HOUSEMAN

Well, I must say this Hamlet may have eight of the most gorgeous court ladies in history.

ANGLE ON HOWARD
smiling in agreement

INT. RESTAURANT
Vivien LEIGH and John GIELGUD talking

GIELGUD

Last night I saw, that long last, the film of *Romeo and Juliet*. That is, I stayed up until the meeting at the ball, which was only about ten minutes in, and then emotion got much the better of me and I retired from a scene of carnage. Unspeakable vulgarity, appalling hamming and utter silliness...

LEIGH

How was Leslie Howard?

GIELGUD

I should not dream of jeering at the acting of either of them, for I didn't wait for them to begin...

INT. NIGHT HOTEL ROOM
Howard and Watts running lines

HOWARD

"Look here upon this picture, and on this,
The counterfeit presentment of two brothers.
See what a grace was seated on this brow..."

ANGLE ON RUTH
entering with newspaper

RUTH

Look at this. (Handing him paper) "John Gielgud has just
accepted an offer to bring his *Hamlet* to Broadway this
season."

HOWARD

(Taking paper) But he said he wasn't going to ... (Reads) I
can't believe this.

RUTH

He's been working on his Hamlet for ten years.

HOWARD

I don't understand.

WATTS

Maybe he wants to show an upstart crow of a movie star
how it's done.

EXT. DAY BOSTON GARDEN
Howard and Houseman walking

HOUSEMAN

Leslie, I urge you to switch from a New York opening
first to a national tour. (Howard frowns) Late in the
spring, the investment recouped, fortified by a national
tour and Gielgud forgotten, you could enter New York
with a virtual assurance of success.

HOWARD

Yes, you're quite right. (Thinks for a moment) Thank you.

> HOUSEMAN
> You need more time to find Hamlet and make him yours.

> HOWARD
> I understand, John. (Looks for a moment at Houseman)
> But we're going to open in New York just as we planned.
> And what will be, will be.

> HOUSEMAN
> (Looking at him for a moment) You are the most
> completely fatalistic man I have ever met.

> HOWARD
> John, don't you see? Gielgud has thrown down a gauntlet.

INT. EVENING THEATER
CLOSE-UP
of the ACTRESS playing Gertrude to a soft spoken Howard

> GERTRUDE
> "O speak to me no more.
> These words like daggers enter in my ears;
> No more sweet Hamlet!"

> HOWARD
> "A murder and a villain,
> A slave that is not twentieth part the tithe
> Of your precedent lord, a vice of kings."

CAMERA CONTINUES TO PULL BACK
to the POV of someone standing in the back of the theater, the
massive grandeur of the 11th century set overwhelming Howard's
delicate, tender and almost inaudible Prince

CLOSE-UP
of Ruth standing there with a look of concern

INT. EVENING HOWARD'S DRESSING ROOM

CLOSE-UP
of newspaper headline above picture of King Edward and Mrs.
Simpson - "Will he give up throne for her?"

HOWARD'S POV
a review inside paper of Gielgud's Hamlet *under headline - "A*
Perfect Performance!" Knock at door

                    HOWARD
Come in.

ANGLE ON DOORWAY
as Oberon enters with DAVID NIVEN, slender young actor not
unlike Howard, in tow

                    OBERON
"One of these days Leslie Howard too will be looked back
on as a great Hamlet."

                    HOWARD
(Smiling faintly) Still reading my notices?

                    OBERON
Always, but a producer's first question is how's the box
office?

                    HOWARD
(Laughing) Passable. (Pause) And how are you?

                    OBERON
Tolerable. (Suddenly) I want you to meet a friend of mine
and an admirer of yours. David Niven.

                    HOWARD
Hmm, yes, I've heard about you. Funny fellow. (Smiling
glance at Oberon) Someday you'll be getting all my parts.

                    OBERON
Oh, David's not at all like you. He's happiest when he's

tanned and stripped down to trunks on a beach, running in and out of the surf.

NIVEN

I'm teaching Merle how to snorkel dive.

OBERON

Oh, you should try it, Leslie.

HOWARD

What? Put on one of those mask things? Oh, no. I don't think I'd like that. Give me nightmares. (They exchange a glance)

OBERON

I loved your Hamlet.

NIVEN

Very poetic.

HOWARD

Thank you. Have you seen...the other one?

NIVEN

Not yet.

OBERON

I thought yours was wonderfully natural, "beautifully repressed" someone said, but...I couldn't always hear you.

HOWARD

Yes, people are telling me I must be bigger...but I don't know...

OBERON

See? You're a born Hamlet. (She stares at him with hard, merry eyes) Can't make up your mind.

ANGLE ON DOORWAY
as Ruth, entering with Doodie, is taken aback by the sight of

Oberon

ANGLE ON HOWARD
as he smiles, startled

> HOWARD
> Oh, hello darling. This is my wife Ruth and my daughter
> Doodie. Merle, David. (Uncomfortable silence)

> OBERON
> We were just discussing Hamlet's inability to make up his
> mind.

> HOWARD
> (After an awkward pause, glancing at headline) King
> Edward's in the same pickle.

> NIVEN
> (Helping Howard out) The American papers are full of it
> but in England there's hardly a word.

> HOWARD
> Ah, the power of the press. It's not what they report. It's
> what they don't report. I'm writing a play on that theme.

> OBERON
> (Not letting go) Do you think a divorced woman is good
> enough for the king?

> HOWARD
> Churchill does. (Imitating Churchill) Let the Prince
> choose his girl.

> OBERON
> There's one vote.

> HOWARD
> (Nervous) King and Country, you know, that's about all
> the religion Winston has. (Ruth remains silent, Howard
> turns to Niven) I played the best friend of a prince who

falls for an American girl...but gives her up for old King and Country. (To Ruth) Remember, dear?

RUTH
(Looking right at Oberon) And that's just what this Prince should do.

OBERON
Why? Is life a stage play?

RUTH
Perhaps, for a king, and even movie stars have to maintain some standards. (Strained silence all around, Doodie looking up wonderingly)

Scene 16 - New York, Opening Night, November 1936

INT. EVENING THEATER
Howard's opening night

ANGLE ON RUTH AND CHILDREN
watching anxiously while a MAN behind them turns to whisper something in the ear of the WOMAN he is with

CROSS CUT
with JOHN GIELGUD in his Hamlet

MONTAGE
cuts between highlights of both, from opening to sword fight and death - Gielgud is vibrant, unpredictable, Howard quiet, almost constrained

HOWARD
"To be, or not the be, that is the question:
Whether'tis nobler in the mind to suffer
The slings and arrows of outrages fortune
Or to take arms against a sea of troubles."

GIELGUD
"And by opposing end them. To die, to sleep-

No more; and by sleep to say we end
The heartache, and the thousand natural shocks
That flesh is heir to."

HOWARD
"Tis a consumation
Devoutly to be wished- to die, to sleep..."

GIELGUD
"To sleep, perchance to dream, ay there`s the rub..."

CURTAIN CALLS
warm applause

ANGLE ON HOWARD
smiling and tired

ANGLE ON RUTH
applauding loudly, Doodie and Wink whistling and stomping

ANGLE ON THE COUPLE
behind Ruth rising

MAN
(To his companion) More an antique Romeo than a Dane.
(They laugh)

INT. EVENING BACK SEAT OF CAB
Oberon reading out loud to Niven

OBERON
"To say that Mr. Howard is a pleasant actor, a charming
fellow, with few equals at the lightly romantic stuff he has
become famous for, explains his popularity without
offering any reason why he should undertake one of the
theater's great roles." (Sighs and looks at Niven) A year
ago he owned Broadway.

INT. NIGHT HOTEL ROOM
Ruth, alone with Howard, reads reviews

RUTH

The Times commends your integrity of spirit and
personal courage...but... (Pause as she stops reading)

HOWARD

(Reading from another paper) It's 'Hamlet with the Hamlet
left out..." (Pause) "Gielgud should feel free to drop the
Giel from his name as his is the Gud Hamlet." (Laughs
dryly) Very clever.

RUTH

You were tired, distracted...

HOWARD

Perhaps, but that doesn't matter now. I'll announce to the
cast that there will be no second night.

RUTH

(Rising) Leslie, you can't!

HOWARD

There's no point in dragging out the agony.

RUTH

Leslie, you can't let them defeat you. You mustn't, not
now, not after all this work. You can't let them have the
final word. Think of your pride.

HOWARD

A life in the theater is one long humiliation. (Pause) Why
go on? (He stares blankly, Ruth wonders what to do,
suddenly smiles)

RUTH

You can't quit now, you're the producer and this turkey
cost a fortune. (He looks at her and they both burst into
laughter)

HOWARD

Right you are, old girl! They shan't have my good name or
my purse! (They continue to laugh together) I defy them!

Scene 17 - New York, performing *Hamlet*, Nov./Dec. 1936

INT. EVENING THEATER
Howard playing to a rapt, if somewhat partisan, audience

DISSOLVE TO CURTAIN CALLS
the applause long and encouraging

MONTAGE
of both Hamlets, ever longer lines under each marquee

EXT. AFTERNOON NEW YORK STREET
as Gielgud settles into backseat of a cab

> GEILGUD
> The Empire Theater, please.

ANGLE ON CAB DRIVER
looking him over

> DRIVER
> Which Hamlet are you?

Gielgud laughs

Scene 18 - New York, December 11, 1936

INT. AFTERNOON HOTEL SUITE
Howard and Ruth listening to Edward's abdication speech on the radio

> KING EDWARD VIII
> ...still I have been denied the one matchless blessing, enjoyed by so many of you and not bestowed on me - a happy home with his wife and children...

ANGLE ON HOWARD
as he glances at Ruth

KING EDWARD VIII
...I have found it impossible to carry the heavy burden of
responsibility and to discharge my duties as King as I
would wish to do without the help and support of the
woman I love.

ANGLE ON RUTH

RUTH
Then it's a good thing.

HOWARD
Hmmm. One tragedy for certain. This affair has ruined all
the anti-Nazi work Winston had accomplished. Siding
with the King may have finished him off politically.

RUTH
There it is.

HOWARD
Yes. Winston's star has come almost as low as mine.

RUTH
(Lovingly) The national tour will recoup our investment,
you'll see. And we'll be working together again...like in
the old days.

Scene 19 - On tour (Kansas City, Los Angeles, etc), 1937

MONTAGE
of trains and performances, a smiling Ruth in the middle of a
traveling circus atmosphere

DISSOLVE TO THE GRAVEYARD SCENE
as Howard holds the skull, he glances down through the opened
grave to a sea of heads and cigarette smoke - the cast and crew
under the stage

ANGLE ON BACK OF RUTH'S HEAD
bobbing happily

EXT. NIGHT CITY SKYLINE
"Kansas City Arms" flashing in neon

DISSOLVE TO INT. HOTEL ROOM
Howard nursing Ruth over a bout with pneumonia, feeding her hot
soup with a spoon

RUTH
You're so good to me.

HOWARD
It's our anniversary. Remember? "Yours, if you want me.
Leslie."

CAMERA PANS TO WINDOW
as they look out over the vast American prairie

HOWARD
This is a hell of a place for it, darling, but we're still going
strong. The best is yet to be.

CAMERA PANS
vast open spaces outside window, stars shinning above

EXT. EVENING LOS ANGELES SKYLINE

INT. RADIO STUDIO
Howard sitting with INTERVIEWER

HOWARD
I must say I've been changed by my experience with
Hamlet.
INTERVIEWER
How so?

HOWARD
Like the Prince I want to produce plays of my own, but I
intend to delay as little as possible. I'll be off to England to
produce one soon.

78

INTERVIEWER
A play you've written?

HOWARD
Yes, called *Alias Mrs. Jones.* It's an attack on the unlimited power of the press barons to suppress and control the news.

INTERVIEWER
(Slightly startled) Oh.

Scene 20 - New York, 1937

*EXT. NIGHT NEW YORK SKYLINE
INT. BOOTH AT SARDI'S
Watts and Howard deep in discussion*

HOWARD
So you're saying the establishment press controls not only our news but our history?

WATTS
History is news. And Shakespeare's plays are, as he says, "the abstracts and brief chronicles of their time."

HOWARD
You see Hamlet as a portrait of the author literally?

WATTS
He is the author. Look at this. (Spreads out a book)

*CLOSE-UP
of the Droeshout engraving of Shakespeare*

WATTS
This is the only official portrait we have of Shakespeare, right?

HOWARD
Correct.

                    WATTS
    What do you think of it?

ANGLE ON HOWARD
squinting skeptically

                    HOWARD
    Hmmm. It does look rather odd. I've always thought that.

                    WATTS
    Like the face is floating above the ruff?

                    HOWARD
    Yes, it does give that impression.

ANGLE ON ENGRAVING

                    WATTS
    And yet it's stranger than that. It has two right eyes. And
    there are to left sides to the coat. See? This is actually a
    <u>rear</u> view of the left shoulder. And this line along the
    neck, that isn't the jaw line. This shadow is.

ANGLE ON HOWARD

                    HOWARD
    How very odd indeed!

                    WATTS
    It's more than odd, it's intentional. This portrait is a one-
    eyed jack, a mask.

                    HOWARD
    Perhaps...

                    WATTS
    I know I'm right. This is the <u>only</u> official portrait and it's a
    phoney. The true author lies concealed under this Stratford
    front.

HOWARD
All right, something's rotten, maybe. But why?

WATTS
Politics. (Pause) Look at Shakespeare's main subjects.
Kings and queens, princes, the ruling class, and always
written from their point of view.

HOWARD
You're not going to say he's Bacon, are you?

WATTS
Bacon? No. This whole debate has changed because of
this book. It's called *Shakespeare Identified*, and the man
it identifies as Shakespeare is the living Elizabethan image
of Hamlet. Edward de Vere, 17th Earl of Oxford,

HOWARD
Really?

WATTS
A courtier close to Queen Elizabeth his whole life.

HOWARD
(With surprised interest) Really?

WATTS
You should just read this book, and then we can talk some
more.

HOWARD
Well, you've got my attention. Let me have it. Anyway, I
need to get going. I'll call you from England. Pascal wants
me to play Higgins.

Scene 21 - London, winter 1938

EXT. DAY LONDON SKYLINE

INT. DAY PASCAL'S OFFICE

ANGLE ON A BEAUTIFUL YOUNG WOMAN, VIOLETTE
CUNNINGTON
watering a plant in the window

CLOSE-UP
as she looks up smiling with large intelligent eyes

ANGLE ON HOWARD'S FACE
slightly awed by her radiant beauty in the sunlight

                    HOWARD
Hello...I'm....

                    VIOLETTE
(With light French accent) You're Leslie Howard. We've
been expecting you. I'm Violette Cunnington, Mr. Pascal's
personal assistant. Make yourself comfortable.

                    HOWARD
Thank you. (He settles into an easy chair)

                    VIOLETTE
I was sorry to miss your Hamlet.

                    HOWARD
(Just a little bit stiffly) Hum...well, by the time I got to the
Coast I was playing the Hamlet I envisioned. (Pause)

                    VIOLETTE
(Feeling a wave of pity and admiration) I think acting is
such a vulnerable profession. One must be very brave.

                    HOWARD
Acting... (He changes course) ... is a silly business, all that
paint and posing, buttering up to producers for jobs and to
the press to persuade the public to want to see your work.
Ugh!

                    VIOLETTE
I should think you would like it. It's what you do.

HOWARD

It's what they pay me for. (In the silence she ponders him)

VIOLETTE

(Quietly curious) Do you want to play Higgins?

HOWARD

Oh, *Pygmalion* is a great play and it's a great part. Beautiful theme, too. Civilizing someone through language. Reminds me of Shakespeare's effect. (Pause, they smile at each other) But... (Glancing at desk piled high with actor's photos) ...who else do they have in mind?

VIOLETTE

Shaw likes Charles Laughton.

CLOSE-UP
of a publicity shot of the fleshy Laughton as Captain Bligh

HOWARD

He'd be fine.

VIOLETTE

Of course, someone with intelligence and sex appeal would be nice too. (Howard shrugs) But it's not what you'd really like, is it?

HOWARD

No.

VIOLETTE

What would you really like?

HOWARD

To direct. That means more to me now than all the rest of this rigmarole. (Looking her in the eyes, gently ironic) An actor is so vulnerable.

ANGLE ON INNER OFFICE DOOR OPENING
GABRIEL PASCAL, a man with a "face like an elephant's behind,"

enters

PASCAL

Leslie, how good to see you! I see you've met Violette.

HOWARD

We've been having a lovely chat. (Pascal glances at
Violette, who signals discreetly that Howard is restive) So,
how do you like England?

PASCAL

Very much. A great nation. As you can see, I've followed
Alex to the promised land. You've inspired us all.

HOWARD

(To Violette's puzzled smile) Like Gabriel and Korda, I'm
just another Hungarian Jew trying to make good in
England.

PASCAL

So, how is Alex?

HOWARD

He's fine. In fact I'm having lunch with him and Winston
this afternoon. I'll give him your best. (Pause)

PASCAL

How is Merle?

HOWARD

Good, I suppose. She's in love with an actor.

PASCAL

Actors! (To Violette) Stay away from actors.

HOWARD

Sound advice.

PASCAL

Yes, yes. (Pause) And how did your *Alias* play do?

HOWARD

Not very well, thank you.

PASCAL

That's what you get for attacking the press.

HOWARD

That's what you get.

PASCAL

Well, never mind that. Have you given any thought to
Higgins?

HOWARD

Some. (Glances at photo on desk) Who else do you have
in mind?

PASCAL

Shaw wants Laughton. Can you imagine? Face like an
elephant's behind.

HOWARD

(He stares at Pascal face for a moment, Violette almost
laughs) He'd be excellent.

PASCAL

True, but you'd be perfect. Can't think of anyone better.

HOWARD

Well, of course I'm flattered. But before I could agree to
play Higgins I need something else.

PASCAL

What?

HOWARD

I want to direct the film.

PASCAL

(Stunned silence, Pascal looks about him, looks at

Violette, who signals he's serious) But I've already offered
it to Anthony Asquith.

HOWARD
(After a moment) Anthony is first rate, I agree. (Pause)

PASCAL
He's accepted. It's signed and sealed.

HOWARD
(He thinks) Let me co-direct and it's a deal. (Pascal looks
at him appraisingly) Gabriel, I'm serious. I'd rather direct
somewhere else, now, than play Higgins. Let Laughton
have it. (Pause)

PASCAL
(Glances at Violette) No, no, it's a deal. (They shake
hands)

HOWARD
(To Violette, looking at photo) Pity, though. Did you
know that Laughton is also Winston's favorite actor?
(With a mischievous wink) Can't imagine why?

CLOSE-UP
of LAUGHTON'S face in photo

Scene 22 - London, winter 1938

DISSOLVE from LAUGHTON'S face to close-up
of WINSTON CHURCHILL'S face

INT. LONDON MEN'S CLUB
Slow pan to CHURCHILL's hand clutching a cigar and brandy
glass, pointing out the scenes in two oil paintings of famous sea
battles

CHURCHILL
There's something about the Continent that breeds political
fanaticism. First came Philip of Spain and his mighty

Armada, beat them, and then Napoleon's fleet at Trafalgar, Nelson took care of that, and now <u>we'll</u> have to take of this Hitler and his gang.

ANGLE ON HOWARD
with ANTHONY EDEN and ALEXANDER KORDA in leather easy chairs, drinks in hand

                    EDEN
No country is so vulnerable as our own. We are rich and easy prey.

                    HOWARD
I hear some of our aristocracy even <u>like</u> Hitler.

                    CHURCHILL
And support him. Traitors. For it will come to war with this guttersnipe.

                    KORDA
We must be ready. We must continue sounding the alarm.

                    CHURCHILL
Yes, something to snap this country awake. Most Englishmen are still as complacent as cows. But these Nazis, God knows, <u>they</u> understand the value of good propaganda. Did you know all SS men are shown *Lives of a Bengal Lancer* because it depicts a handful of Englishmen holding a continent in thrall?

                    HOWARD
How flattering!

                    CHURCHILL
Yes, that's the Germans for you. Either at your throat or at your feet.

                    EDEN
They even think Shakespeare was German!

HOWARD

How odd you should say that. I've been doing a lot of thinking about the Shakespeare problem.

CHURCHILL

What problem?

HOWARD

Well, you know, the question of whether it really could have been the Stratford man. There are some ...

CHURCHILL

(Interrupting) Leslie, there is no Shakespeare problem. Just a nonsense problem.

EDEN

Don't we have more important things to worry about right now?

HOWARD

But, really, whose nonsense? Why should Shakespeare be such a mystery? Because he is, you know. No one really can explain how this fellow burst forth from total obscurity to do what he did. We know that.

CHURCHILL

You can't explain genius, Leslie. Shakespeare belonged to his time the way Jesus did to his. It produced him, but it can't explain him.

HOWARD

That's no answer.

CHURCHILL

(Firmly) We have his works and the rest is not worth discussing. (Silence)

HOWARD

Well, I see. (Pause)

EDEN

Anyway, as you were saying, the press will have it's way. I s
till think it's a shame what they did to the King.

CHURCHILL

Disgraceful.

EDEN

But he showed what he was made of in his farewell. It was a
great speech.

CHURCHILL

(Without apparent irony) It should be. I wrote it.

CLOSE-UP
HOWARD studiously looking at CHURCHILL

Scene 23 - London, winter 1938

*CAMERA PULLS BACK TO INT. NIGHT HOWARD'S HOTEL
SUITE*
Howard on phone, examining Droeshout portrait in Shakespeare
Identified.

HOWARD

Your book was fascinating. It's almost like you can reach
out and touch him.

ANGLE ON WATTS
in New York apartment

WATTS

And what do you think of Oxford?

HOWARD

Very curious fellow.

WATTS

I know. Edward De Vere is remembered in history as an
inconsequential fop, a sort of Scarlet Pimpernel. (Howard

nods) In reality, he was Hamlet.

HOWARD

Yes, I can see that. A prince of the realm, denied political power, putting on plays to expose the court's corruption. Protected by the Queen.

WATTS

In Oxford's case, your Virgin Queen. You see? The hoax was set up to protect her. How could the character of Gertrude ever be reconciled with the national myth of a Virgin Queen?

HOWARD

(Laughing) Yes, it all sounds like an improbable heresy.

WATTS

But the play's the thing, you see? They had to be severed from reality. That's why Shakespeare's such a mystery.

HOWARD

How many other people are aware of all this?

WATTS

Well, it's been growing quite rapidly in some circles. But the real powers that be want no part of it. It's dynamite.

HOWARD

Yes, yes. It really upsets a whole lot of apple carts, doesn't it.

WATTS

Apple carts are the least of it.

Scene 24 - Austria, winter 1938

EXT. DAY ALPS PANORAMA
tiny figures skiing down snow covered slopes

MEDIUM SHOT

Howard, Doodie and Violette racing down a trail, laughing.
Violette falling at the bottom of the run. Ruth and Pascal watching
and laughing. Howard helps her to her feet, holds her a moment too
long.

ANGLE ON RUTH AND PASCAL
watching, a trace of anxiety fleeting across their faces

INT. NIGHT LODGE BAR
the family sitting around a table, Howard next to Violette, as Pascal
approaches with ALFONS WALDE, a tall, handsome man

> PASCAL
> Leslie, this is Alfons Walde, the painter.

> HOWARD
> Delighted to meet you. Much admired that canvas I saw of
> yours.

> WALDE
> If you like, I would be honored to have you visit my studio.

INT. DAY WALDE'S STUDIO
Howard admiring a beautiful view of the mountains thru a large
picture window

> WALDE
> Of course, Austria is finished as an independent country.

> HOWARD
> Is that your sense of it?

> WALDE
> It's only a matter of time before Hitler crosses the border.
> (He glances about the room at his expressionist sketches and
> murals) We'll soon be straight-jacketed.

> HOWARD
> Yes, no more of this stuff.

WALDE

(Nodding, appraising his work) Too free, too decadent...
(Pause) ... too Jewish. Dr. Goebbels will never stand for this.

HOWARD

Will you be able to make a living?

WALDE

Many artists, professors, even pastors have been discharged
already for "intellectual aberrations," racial impurity or
simply refusing to genuflect before the Fuhrer. Others have
just disappeared...

HOWARD

Disappeared?

WALDE

One day you go to see them and they are gone, no one
knows where. And nothing happens. The papers, the
authorities, even the neighbors, are silent.

HOWARD

My God.

ANGLE ON WALDE

WALDE

There is no law, these people are gangsters. I have many
good friends here, this is where I grew up, but within weeks
we'll have new masters - and then... it will be a little
unstable.

HOWARD

What will you do?

WALDE

I don't know. This is my home. But I may have to get out...
(grim smile)...or go into the cage with the other wild beasts.

> HOWARD
>
> Is there anything I can do?

> WALDE
>
> For us, now, there is very little anyone can do. (Pause) You can tell people what is happening. England must know, they must understand what we are facing.

ANGLE ON HOWARD
as he slowly nods his head

Scene 25 - Outside London, filming *Pygmalion*, March 12, 1938

INT. DAY MOVIE STUDIO
CLOSE-UP OF HOWARD
concentrating

ANGLE ON THE PYGMALION SET
Pascal, Violette, ASQUITH and CREW are all watching him film a scene with WENDY HILLER as Eliza

ANGLE ON HOWARD AND HILLER
as he pops a chocolate in her mouth

> HOWARD
>
> "Now, Eliza, speak clearly."

> HILLER
>
> "The shallow depressions in the west of these islands are moving in a westerly direction."

> HOWARD
>
> "Terrible." (Pops another in her mouth) "Now try again."

> HILLER
>
> "The shallow depressions..." (She gasps) Oh, my, I've swallowed one, Leslie!

> HOWARD
>
> That's all right, we've plenty more.

ANGLE ON THE SET
as everyone cracks-up at Howard's ad-lib

ANGLE ON VIOLETTE
laughing with pure, unaffected pleasure and admiration

ASQUITH
Very funny, Leslie. Maybe we should leave that one in.

ANGLE ON A YOUNG MAN
entering with a worried look on his face

YOUNG MAN
It just came over the radio. Hitler's storm troopers have
marched into Austria.

ANGLE ON HOWARD
the smile on his face turning to shock and sadness

Scene 26 - London, 1938

INT. NIGHT BEDROOM
DREAM SEQUENCE
Howard is staring at the Droeshout portrait as it's features drift off
like the layers of a mask until beneath is revealed the tragic gaze of
Oxford, his face bringing the portrait to life and color

ANGLE ON HOWARD
as he snaps fully awake and blinks at his familiar room and his own
ghostly face in the night darkened window

INT. EVENING RESTAURANT
Howard and Violette sitting across from each other, silently falling in
love

HOWARD
It's impossible to raise money on an anti-Nazi film. Nobody's
interested. Don't want to offend the Germans, you know.

VIOLETTE
I like your "Bonnie Prince Charlie" script.

HOWARD
Yes, I've always been attracted to that rather touching fellow and his forlorn hope.

VIOLETTE
The man who would be king. Another Hamlet.

HOWARD
English history is full of such stories. (He regards her for a moment) In fact, I've been reading up on a fellow named Edward De Vere. (She smiles) The Earl of Oxford.

VIOLETTE
Oxford? The one who is supposed to be Shakespeare?

HOWARD
I'm pretty nearly convinced he <u>was</u> Shakespeare...or at least a hidden Hamlet.

VIOLETTE
That might make a good movie.

HOWARD
Hmmm. I'd have to raise money in <u>Germany</u> to make that one. (He smiles at her. She laughs lightly, with a blush)

Scene 27 - Pinewood Studios, filming *Pygmalion*, 1938

MONTAGE
of filming Pygmalion, *Howard and Asquith behind camera, checking shot, then Howard walking in front to play scene, Pascal nodding in approval, Violette watching with admiration*
INT. DAY MOVIE STUDIO
final day on the set, final shot

ANGLE ON PASCAL
beaming at Howard

PASCAL
Beautiful job, Leslie. You should get an Oscar for this one.

HOWARD
I think I've got what I want. (Winks at Violette)

INT. DAY PASCAL'S OFFICE
ANGLE ON PASCAL
no longer beaming

PASCAL
I knew it! I knew something was going on. You're making a
mistake, Violette. Leslie is a beautiful guy, there's no
denying, but he's faithless. Look what he did to Oberon.

VIOLETTE
He has not offered me a job as his mistress.

PASCAL
He will.

VIOLETTE
Gabriel... (Pause)

PASCAL
Sure, go ahead. What do I have to say about it?

INT. DAY HOWARD'S OFFICE

CLOSE-UP OF A NOVEL COVER
The Man Who Lost Himself *by H. de Vere Stacpoole, with a drawing*
of a haunted looking hero

ANGLE ON VIOLETTE
looking up from it, smiling

HOWARD
What do you think of it as a film? A commoner who must
switch identities with a nobleman, who then dies, leaving the
imposter to live out his troubled life.

VIOLETTE
Well, I think you've found yourself another Hamlet. But the name is really too wonderful. De Vere.

HOWARD
I wonder if he's a descendent? (Pause. He comes up to her) You really are wonderful. (He kisses her, very gently but fully on her lips, at first she does not respond, but he is so tender and light that soon she is seeking his lips back)

Scene 28 - Stowe Maries, London, Paris, 1938

EXT. DAY STOWE MARIES' GARDEN
as the novel is being shoved across a table

ANGLE ON HOWARD AND RUTH
sitting at breakfast in their garden

RUTH
(Pushing it away) Leslie, I don't think playing these sordid types will do much to enhance your reputation. Won't you be somewhat out of character?

HOWARD
Really, Ruth, must you take such a limited view.

RUTH
I just think there's something more important you could be doing.

HOWARD
Of course.

RUTH
I'm sorry, Leslie. I just don't know what attracts you to these stories.

INT. NIGHT HOWARD'S OFFICE
lights low, Howard and Violette entwined on sofa, speaking softly

HOWARD
I love you.

VIOLETTE
And I love you... (She stops, pulls her head back) What are we doing? I love you, I do... (She looks at him) ...but...

HOWARD
(Understanding) But I'm married... (Long silence)

VIOLETTE
Leslie, we both need to think, now, before it hurts too much...

EXT. EVENING FOGGY AIRPORT
Howard, in trench coat and hat, and Violette at the boarding gate, a DC-3 on runway, engines turning

HOWARD
Remember me... (He reaches to kiss her)

VIOLETTE
People may be watching. (He pauses, then continues to her mouth, which he kisses fully and slowly, she breaks away and rushes to the plane)

ANGLE ON HOWARD
as he watches the DC-3 take off

DISSOLVE TO EXT. DAY PARIS
Violette strolling by the River Seine

HOWARD (Voice over)
...and as you went I knew my life was in the airplane with you.

EXT. DAY LONDON
Howard looking out over the River Thames

VIOLETTE (Voice over)
Paris is so beautiful but all I think of is you...

EXT. DAY PARIS
Violette standing on a bridge over the river

> HOWARD (Voice over)
> I realize now that despite all the pain it will cause I don't
> want to go on without you. Please, return...

EXT. AFTERNOON LONDON AIRPORT
Howard waiting in trench coat, hat drawn over his face, people
disembarking plane

HOWARD'S POV
Violette emerging from plane, looking around

ANGLE ON HOWARD
his face lighting up while he remains discreet, people brushing past
him

ANGLE ON VIOLETTE
she waves

ANGLE ON HOWARD
as they greet each other quietly, without open displays of affection

INT. NIGHT HOTEL ROOM
Howard is laying in Violette's arms in bed

> HOWARD
> I really want to get the *Man Who Lost Himself* off the ground.
> It's just trashy enough to raise money on.

> VIOLETTE
> There's always been a market for noblemen with mixed-up
> identities. (Laughs knowingly)

> HOWARD
> Someday, when I have the power, I'll make a movie about the
> real Hamlet. But right now, well, RKO has asked me to New
> York to have discussions about this project...and I want you
> do go with me. (Pause, she looks at him) Ruth'll stay home

with the children.

Scene 29 - Sailing back to United States, fall 1938

EXT. DAY SHIP'S DOCK
the Normandie is about to sail

ANGLE ON HOWARD
saying good-bye to Ruth and children

ANGLE ON HOWARD
climbing gang plank, waving to them innocently

HOWARD'S POV
his family waving back to him

SHIP BOARD MONTAGE
Howard searching thru the crowd for Violette but not finding her

INT. SHIP'S CORRIDOR
Howard still looking as he heads towards his room

INT. HOWARD'S CABIN
disconsolate, he stands there, surrounded by his luggage, as the
ship's siren booms

ANGLE ON HOWARD
Standing alone in the awful stillness, then a knock at the door

> HOWARD
Yes?

ANGLE ON CABIN DOOR
as it opens and she is standing there

> VIOLETTE
> I was lost. (She walks into his waiting arms)

> HOWARD
> (Kissing and embracing her) I thought something must have

gone wrong with the rendezvous. You had missed the boat -
mistaken the date...something awful had happened!

                    VIOLETTE
No, no...

                    HOWARD
Or that you'd lost your nerve, changed your mind, decided
the whole thing was too ridiculous... (Tears in his eyes)

                    VIOLETTE
It is too ridiculous. (She kisses him peacefully)

EXT. DAY OCEAN HORIZON
Ship steaming along

Scene 30 - New York, traveling to California, fall 1938

DISSOLVE TO NEW YORK SKYLINE
INT. NIGHT HOTEL ROOM
high above the city, Howard lying on couch as Violette hands him a
telegram
                    VIOLETTE
They want you to play Ashley Wilkes in *Gone With The*
Wind.

                    HOWARD
Who's he? (She hands him an enormous script, which he eyes
skeptically)

EXT. DAY PRAIRIE HORIZON
train crossing slowly

ANGLE ON HOWARD AND VIOLETTE
deeply in love, looking out the window at the rolling countryside
reflected in the glass

EXT. DAY CALIFORNIA ORANGE GROVES
train crossing in background

ANGLE ON HOWARD AND VIOLETTE
standing on rear observation platform of train, she leaning against
his chest, his arms around her, the wind whipping them

VIOLETTE
Hmmm...? What's that?

HOWARD
(Smelling her hair) Orange blossoms...they were in bloom the
first time I crossed America.

INT. SLEEPING CAR ON TRAIN - NIGHT
a little later, Howard and Violette asleep in bed together Howard
tosses and turns, then yells out and sits up abruptly.

VIOLETTE
Leslie, Leslie! What's the matter? Are you alright?

HOWARD
Yes, Yes. I'm fine (Pauses, breathing deeply). It's just a bad
dream about the war. They keep happening.

VIOLETTE
You were in those god awful blood-bath battles, weren't you?
I've heard some talk.

HOWARD
No, no. I'm fine (Pauses again, looks at her). It's over, but I
can never get away from it. (Pauses).

VIOLETTE
It can be helpful just to talk sometimes. I'll listen.

HOWARD
(Long pause) Actually, there's not much to tell. (Pauses) I
probably never should have even joined up. It was a big
mistake. Some of us, you know, were never meant to be
soldiers, let alone officers. (Pauses) The simple truth is, I
never got close to a battle, but whenever I was with men who
had I felt (Pauses) ... well, not one of them. (Pauses) So I've

been letting people believe for years that my "breakdown" was from battle stress. (Pauses) Well, it wasn't stress at all (Pauses) ... it was shame. When I got to Paris they sized me up and said I didn't belong on the front, I couldn't handle it. (Pauses) And they were right.

VIOLETTE
Oh, Leslie! (She hugs him.) You didn't want blood on your hands... yours or anyone else's. (They embrace, but HOWARD stares off into space over her shoulder.)

FADE OUT

Scene 31 - Los Angeles, Hollywood, fall 1938

EXT. DAY LOS ANGELES STATION
train pulling in

INT. DAY OFFICE DOOR
with "David Selznick" written on it

DISSOLVE TO MEETING
still in progress, DAVID SELZNICK and Howard

HOWARD
You know this Ashley fellow really doesn't interest me that much...perhaps David Niven...

SELZNICK
I've got a great part coming up in *Intermezzo*. It's going to be a first class production with an incredibly beautiful new girl from Sweden, Ingrid Bergman. (Shows him a photo of her)

HOWARD
Intermezzo?

SELZNICK
It's a love story about a married man, a world famous conductor, who has an affair with his protegee. (Knowing it's Howard's own) Beautiful story.

HOWARD
Hmmm...sounds intriguing, David, but you know I want to get behind the camera.

SELZNICK
Play Ashley and you'll have the staring role in *Intermezzo*, top billing... (Howard sighs without enthusiasm) And I'll make you an associate producer on it as well.

HOWARD
(Looking up with a smile) Now, that might be the basis for something...but, you know David, I don't really think I can do much with this Ashley fellow.

SELZNICK
Don't <u>do</u> anything, Leslie. Just be yourself.

ANGLE ON HOWARD
frowning

Scene 32 - Beverly Hills, Hollywood, fall 1938

EXT. DAY BEVERLY HILLS
a beautiful Tudor house, a little red roadster drives up, horn honks

ANGLE ON VIOLETTE
coming out the door in tasteful and simple evening gown

ANGLE ON HOWARD
as he jumps out of the car

HOWARD
Well, how do you like it?

VIOLETTE
It's very...sporty.

HOWARD
(With French inflection) Discreet, no?

VIOLETTE
(Laughing, pause) And how am I to be presented at this gala?

HOWARD
If anyone wants to know you are my production assistant
...and let the chips fly where they may.

INT. EVENING HOLLYWOOD PARTY
two orchestras, strings of colored lights, roses, orchids and
gardenias in festoons from the ceilings - every kind of exotic food and
drink - dozens of stars

ANGLE ON VARIOUS FAMOUS FACES
very glamorous Katharine Hepburn, Betty Davis, Gary Cooper, Cary
Grant, etc.

CLOSE-UP OF VIOLETTE
both amused and amazed by the fairytale atmosphere

VIOLETTE
It is a bit like dying and going to heaven.

HOWARD
Yes...it all looks very pretty when you see it this way.

HOWARD'S POV
Bogart laughing, taking a drink.

HOWARD
Ah, there's someone you should meet.

ANGLE ON BOGART
as he looks up, smiles, and excuses himself

ANGLE ON HOWARD
as he smiles at Violette and Bogart joins them

BOGART
Leslie, you old cheapskate, how are you?

HOWARD
Prospering. (They shake hands warmly) This is my personal assistant, Violette Cunnington.

BOGART
(Nodding) You know I owe my career to this guy. He could do the same for you.

VIOLETTE
We'll see.

BOGART
If I ever have a kid I'm going to name him Leslie...

VIOLETTE
(Slightly puzzled by the connection) Oh?

BOGART
...if he's a girl.

HOWARD
Oh? You've added a stipulation?

BOGART
Well, in America, a boy named Leslie...it would be tough.

HOWARD
I think I understand ... (with effete emphasis) Humphrey.

BOGART
(Laughs) You would... (They both laugh. A beautiful BETTE DAVIS comes up behind Howard.)

DAVIS
Hi, Leslie. How's everything?

HOWARD
(Recovering) Oh, it's you. Hello. Violette, this is Bette Davis.

                    DAVIS
(Looking her up and down) Hello.

                    HOWARD
She is my personal assistant.

                    DAVIS
How personal? (Laughs. To Violette) You don't have to
answer that. (Laughs again) Oh, such a little devil. (To
Howard) I heard you were always nibbling away at some
little extra. (Looks over at Bogart.) Is that right, Bogie?

                    BOGART
(Strained) Didn't notice.

                    DAVIS
(To Violette) Enjoy it while it lasts, kid.

ANGLE ON
Violette reacting with surprise and distress

INT. PARTY
Bogart and Howard are drinking by the bar

                    HOWARD
I never cease to be astonished at her incredible frugality.

ANGLE ON VIOLETTE - HOWARD'S POV
she is moving through the overdressed crowd

                    HOWARD
That dinner dress? Picked it up for a song. And for jewelry
she buys a necklet of gilded tin leaves, two and a half dollars!

ANGLE ON BOGART
lighting a cigarette

                    BOGART
She's a rare bird in this business, alright. Given any thought
to what the vultures will make of her? So rare a bird...and no

wife around.

> HOWARD
> You think there'll be talk?

> BOGART
> (Sardonic laugh) Are you kidding? Hollywood is still the smallest town in the world.

ANGLE ON VIOLETTE - HOWARD'S POV
as she comes walking, smiling towards him

Scene 33 - Los Angeles, winter 1939

DISSOLVE TO EXT. DAY TRAIN STATION
HOWARD'S POV
as Doodie, closely followed by Ruth, comes walking towards him, smiling

ANGLE ON HOWARD
as Doodie rushes into his arms, their joyous embrace almost upsetting the bunch of flowers in his hand

ANGLE ON RUTH
as she receives his warm hug

ANGLE ON HAPPY FAMILY
as the press takes pictures

DISSOLVE TO CLOSE-UP
newspaper print of one of these pictures, under headline about him as one of the stars of Gone With The Wind

INT. DAY HOWARD'S FAMILY HOME
ANGLE ON HOWARD
as he admires the picture briefly and turns to Ruth and Doodie

> HOWARD
> Well, I hope Wink is enjoying boarding school more than I am *Gone With The Wind*. (Smacks paper into palm of his

hand)

                    RUTH
Now, Leslie, it can't be that bad.

                    HOWARD
I am not keen about it. Never read the book, but I've read the
script, miles of it, and I don't know what they're all talking
about or what the devil's wrong with them... (Smacks palm
again) ...most of all Ashley.

                    DOODIE
Oh, Dad, you love it. Tea, anyone?

                    RUTH
That would be lovely. (After she's left, Ruth takes the paper
from Howard) It's going to be a very big movie, Leslie. It
will do your career good.

                    HOWARD
Yes, I know, money is the mission here, and who am I to
refuse it? Still, I hate the damn part. (Lowering his voice) I'm
not nearly beautiful or young enough for Ashley, and it
makes me sick being fixed up to look attractive.

                    RUTH
You'll be fine. (With an edge) You always are.

ANGLE ON HOWARD
troubled by her tone, looking up

ANGLE ON RUTH
after a moment, stern and hurt

                    RUTH
        I know about Violette.

ANGLE ON HOWARD
in stunned silence, staring back at her

RUTH

Do you want a divorce? (Pause)

HOWARD

No... (Ruth glances down at newspaper picture)

RUTH

But you won't give her up? (Silence)

HOWARD

(Quietly, firmly) No. (Long silence)

DOODIE

(Calling from kitchen) There's no cream. Is milk good enough?

ANGLE ON HOWARD
glancing down

RUTH

(Calling to Doodie bravely) Milk will do, precious!

Scene 34 - Hollywood, spring 1939

EXT. DAY HOLLYWOOD HILLS
beautiful, windy, dramatic sky under which Howard and Violette ride
on horseback

HOWARD

I've been thinking, before we return to England, I've been having tantalizing dreams of Hawaii, Japan, the Orient...we'd be away from Hollywood, the press...everyone.

VIOLETTE

In France there is an understanding that marriage is a contract and love a private affair. I'm not expecting you to give up your family.

HOWARD

I do love you.

INT. DAY MOVIE SET
of Gone With The Wind. *VIVIEN LEIGH and LAURENCE OLIVIER*
are sitting in folding chairs with Howard, in his Civil War costume,
as a PHOTOGRAPHER snaps their picture, nods and leaves

> HOWARD
>
> How is *Wuthering Heights* going?

> OLIVIER
>
> Not too badly. David Niven's playing a part that would have
> been perfect for you... (Howard laughs) ... just as Merle's role
> would have been perfect for Vivien.

> HOWARD
>
> Yes, we seem to have each others leading ladies. That's
> Hollywood!

> OLIVIER
>
> Merle sends her warmest regards.

> HOWARD
>
> Merle. Dear Merle. How is she?

> OLIVIER
>
> Stunning, of course. You know, she told me the oddest thing.
> She said Korda originally wanted Charles Laughton to play
> the Scarlett Pimpernel.

> HOWARD
>
> Yes. They wanted him for *Pygmalion* too. Too bad they
> didn't want him for this damn thing.

> OLIVIER
>
> I've played a few roles I couldn't really relate to. I'm not like
> Hamlet, really. (An awkward pause, was this a dig?) But
> great parts are cannibals. Acting great parts devours you. It's
> a dangerous game.

> HOWARD
>
> Hamlet was an actor who played a dangerous game. (To

Leigh) By the way, did you look at that book I showed you?

LEIGH
Yes, fascinating. In fact your Oxford reminds me of Ashley...don't you see? The last of a noble line, then gone with the wind. (To Olivier) Larry, did you ever think Shakespeare may not have written Shakespeare?

ANGLE ON OLIVIER
sudden hardness

OLIVIER
(With finality) No, I never did and I'm not about to start now.

ANGLE ON HOWARD AND LEIGH
exchanging a glance of resignation on this chilly reception

MONTAGE
of filming both Gone with the Wind *and* Intermezzo, *closing with wrap parties on both sets*

INT. EVENING EXOTIC HOLLYWOOD BAR
Howard, Violette and Bogart seated at table

HOWARD
(With gentle irony) I have been advised to remain in Hollywood and pursue my flourishing career.

BOGART
You pay taxes to the Republic, not the King, this is where your bread is buttered. Aren't you being a bit chauvinistic, going back and putting your head in the Lion's mouth?

HOWARD
(With a smile) I might even be conscripted.

BOGART
The war to end all wars. (Laughs grimly) Yeah, well, (Lifting his glass in a mock toast) Peace in our time. (Pause) Leslie, stay here. You know what's coming.

Scene 35 - Desert outside Los Angeles, spring 1939

EXT. NIGHT DESERT
Violette and Howard, two small figures standing close together
against the dark immensity of the vast, empty landscape

> HOWARD
> After I arrive in England with Ruth and the family I'll explain
> that I must meet with the producer and writer for *The Man*
> *Who Lost Himself* in the south of France...and rendezvous
> there with you.

> VIOLETTE
> We could drive together to the Mediterranean - through
> Normandy to Paris, visit the village where I was born...

> HOWARD
> We will.

ANGLE ON THEIR FACES
turned upwards in wonder

MOVING SHOT UPWARDS
against the stars, their voices

> VIOLETTE
> (Frightened) We are so small, so unimportant...what does the
> future mean for us? How can we hold together?

> HOWARD
> There's a mystery to our coming together. We can never,
> never part - this is not just for nothing.

INT. NIGHT BEDROOM

Violette and Howard sleeping, he is having his recurrent dream of the
approaching bombs exploding in a line aimed towards him. He jolts
awake. Violette, half asleep, reaches out to caress and calm him. He
lays back, staring at the ceiling

Scene 36 - New York, summer 1939

DISSOLVE TO EXT. NIGHT NEW YORK SKYLINE
INT. TABLE AT SARDI'S
Howard speaking enthusiastically to a subdued Watts

HOWARD
Seeing Oxford as the author changes everything. The plays
become so personal. It seems so silly now, to have been so
literal about setting Hamlet in 11th Century Denmark. As if
that's what he really cared about. It's his relationship with the
Queen, that's the key. It's his world he's describing. It should
be set in his world - or our own. Don't you think?

WATTS
Well, actually, I'm not so sure anymore...

HOWARD
Sure about what?

WATTS
It's just, well, we have the plays, I'm not so sure anymore it's
so important who wrote them.

HOWARD
Of course it is. You know that. (Pause) Why are you saying
this?

WATTS
Well, it's just that, if you're trying to work in a university
with this problem...this subject... (Laughs) I mean, there's a
kind of a curse on this story.

HOWARD
Hmmm...

WATTS
It just gets to look so obvious, I know, but there is no proof
and people hate you for pursuing it.

HOWARD
But you still believe Oxford was the author?

WATTS
That may be what I believe, but unlike you, I'm really not in a position to fight for it. I have to make a living in the academic world. You must know how people, people in authority, react to this question.

HOWARD
Yes, I understand what you're saying.

WATTS
I don't know why, but for some strange reason this question has been demonized. It's forbidden.

Scene 37 - Traveling, London, Stowe Maries, August 1939

EXT. DAY NEW YORK DOCK
Howard and family waving good-bye on the gangplank of an ocean liner as photographers snap pictures

EXT. NIGHT BROADWAY
Violette standing alone at newsstand, looking at picture of Howard and family

INT. EVENING SHIP'S TELEGRAPH OFFICE
Howard standing alone, sending a wire

INSERT CLOSE-UP
of wire:
August 30, 1939.
to Violette Cunnington Ile de France
Guerre inevitable. Descend Plymouth au lieu Havre.
T'attends, t'adore. Leslie

EXT. NIGHT BIG BEN
booming out eleven o'clock

INT. NIGHT LONDON FLAT

Howard and Violette sitting together listening to a dry, pedantic voice on the radio

CHAMBERLAIN'S VOICE
As no reply has been received from Hitler, a state of war now exists between Germany and England.

ANGLE ON HOWARD AND VIOLETTE
looking at each other as the first wail of air-raid sirens begins

INT. EVENING STOWE MARIES
Howard surrounded by his family in living room

DOODIE
Where were you when you heard the news?

HOWARD
(He stares at his daughter for a moment, aware that Ruth's eyes are upon him) I was with Violette. (Pause) In fact, I'll be in town a lot, trying to get this film off the ground. I'll only make it out here on occasional week-ends. (Silence, he sees the disappointment in his daughter's eyes) But home will remain my touchstone. (Silence again)

EXT. DAY BACKYARD
at Stowe Maries as the family stands outside their bomb shelter in gas masks, NEWSPAPER MEN snap photos

INT. NIGHT VIOLETTE'S FLAT
CLOSE-UP
of photo in paper

ANGLE ON VIOLETTE
looking at photo and smiling

HOWARD (Voice)
I'm beginning to feel rather like *The Man Who Lost Himself* myself. Why am I here?

                         VIOLETTE
What's happened?

ANGLE ON HOWARD

                         HOWARD
Hollywood won't shoot in England. They want me back
there.

                         VIOLETTE
Do you want to go back?

                         HOWARD
Contract or no contract, I'm staying here.

                         VIOLETTE
Then we'll make the film here.

                         HOWARD
That won't be so easy. There's no money in England for
commercial films. (Pause) I'm going to have to come up with
a more timely idea than *The Man Who Lost Himself.*

EXT. DAY WHITEHALL
Howard entering

INT. DAY OFFICE
CLOSE-UP OF WHITEHALL OFFICIAL

                         OFFICIAL
All I see is obstacles, there's rationing, manpower, materials,
petrol, the whole show. We're trying to get organized to fight
a war.

ANGLE ON HOWARD
impatient grimace
                         OFFICIAL
Look, we've never been awfully successful at making films in
peacetime and to start now in war-time seems crazy to me.
(Sighs deeply) I can't help you.

INT. MORNING STOWE MARIES
Howard, Wink, Doodie and Ruth at breakfast

> RUTH
> It's two different minds, the warmly imaginative against the coldly rational. The civil service and you don't mix. When did art ever mix with government?

> HOWARD
> They've mixed. Shakespeare was England's first Minister of Propaganda. (Silence, the others glance at each other) Still a plan should be drawn up for England's use of her entertainment industry in this crisis.

> RUTH
> Then you should do it and take it directly to the top.

Scene 38 - London, September 1939

INT. DAY HEADQUARTER'S - BRITISH INTELLIGENCE
Communications room, radio transmitters all around,
INTERPRETERS listening, constant murmur of radio voices

ANGLE ON ANTHONY EDEN
speaking with Howard

> EDEN
> We're monitoring the last free broadcasts out of Poland.

ANGLE ON POLISH TRANSLATOR
hunched over a receiver, listening to his countrymen voice, taking notes

ANGLE ON HOWARD
nodding as Eden speaks

> EDEN
> I read your manifesto covering home and overseas propaganda. Very interesting. Reaching the Americans will be very important.

HOWARD

With the Americans we must be very careful. No mention of them fighting at our side. They must simply be shown that with nothing to gain we have undertaken the cause of Poland, simply because we cannot stand by and see her dominated by a bully. (Suddenly the room goes quiet)

ANGLE ON TRANSLATOR
as he looks by from his silent radio

ANGLE ON HOWARD AND EDEN
listening to silence

ANGLE ON TRANSLATOR
as a German voice comes on, the translator looks away

Scene 39 - London, September 1939

EXT. DUSK TERRACE OF VIOLETTE'S FLAT
Howard, smoking his pipe, and Violette against a vast panorama of London skyline

HOWARD

I wonder about the artist we met in Austria. Where is he now?

VIOLETTE

Silenced too. (Pause)

HOWARD

I feel so helpless.

VIOLETTE

France will be next. Hitler is going to have his own Reign of Terror.

HOWARD

Yes, the man with a million guillotines. (Pause as they look at each other, Violette smiles)

VIOLETTE
(Softly) Pimpernel. (Howard nods)

HOWARD
A modern Pimpernel...

VIOLETTE
...saving people from the Nazis.

HOWARD
Yes, yes...it could be a straight forward adventure tale...a rescue story.

VIOLETTE
Like Pimpernel he outsmarts them.

HOWARD
Yes, deception. A double identity. But what would be his cover? Nothing fancy. Not someone who would draw attention to himself. (As he pulls on his pipe, deep in thought, Violette looks at him)

VIOLETTE
(French-cockney accent) 'E could be a professor.

Scene 40 - Stowe Maries, London, fall 1939

INT. EVENING STOWE MARIES
Howard, Ruth, Wink and Doodie at the dinner table

HOWARD
He'll be an archaeology professor at Oxford, a scholarly though absent-minded sort who has the habit of taking his students on long vacations to various countries for "digs."

WINK
What are you going to call him? (Howard shrugs)

RUTH
Why not Pimpernel? It would be good box-office.

HOWARD

I've been thinking I'd just call him Smith. (Seeing the look of disappointment flash across her face) Pimpernel Smith. (Laugher) But you're right, dear. The problem, of course, will be money.

MONTAGE
of Howard in London, making rounds, talking in the offices of
MONEY PEOPLE

INT. NIGHT STOWE MARIES
Howard pacing in front of Ruth, Wink and Doodie

HOWARD

(To Ruth) We've already added a romantic interlude, just as make weight for the box- office. And they're charming, these backers, absolutely charming, they show burning enthusiasm. Then, they back out!

MONTAGE
of Howard traveling, having discussions

INT. DAY LONDON PUB
Howard and Violette having drinks at a table

HOWARD

I've learned one thing. In the early stages of negotiations <u>seem</u> prepared to make radical changes, without the slightest intention of abiding by them. I'm learning to be devious. It's the only language they understand.

VIOLETTE

Why not try the British Counsel again? They're in charge of propaganda for the war effort.

INT. DAY LONDON RESTAURANT
Howard with Violette, Wink and Doodie at a table

HOWARD

The British Council has arranged an invitation from the

Anglo French Propaganda Council for me and Violette to
visit British General Headquarters in Paris this April.

WINK
(To Violette) Paris. It'll be like going home for you.

VIOLETTE
Yes, we are very hopeful.

Scene 41 - Paris, London, winter 1940

EXT. DAY PLANE LANDING IN PARIS
EXT. DAY PARIS
*Howard and Violette as they walk slowly up the Champs Elysees from
the Rond Point to the Arc de Triomphe*

EXT. SUNSET PARIS
*as they marvel at the setting sun, the soft warm air, the lovers
shuffling along the gravel sidewalks, seemingly drugged into a
complacent ignoring of the great crisis*

VIOLETTE
It's almost as if Hitler were giving us a chance to think again,
to change out minds about a war we might reasonably
consider an error of judgement.

HOWARD
Yes, and then come back for us later. (Tapping out his pipe) I
suppose we should be preparing for the worst. I've learned
that Alexander Korda is moving to America to do undercover
work for the top man there. (Smiles) He'll use his film
production office as a front. Even Merle is acting as a courier
and informant. (Silence)

VIOLETTE
And what will you be doing?

HOWARD
I've become what the Germans call a V-Person. Part time,
unpaid, "friend" to the secret service."

VIOLETTE
Which means?

HOWARD
Oh, nothing much. Propaganda mostly. My main bit will be the celuoid adventures of Professor Smith... (Seeing the worried look in her eyes) ...Smith...doesn't quite ring, does it? How about Mister V? For Vere, truth.

VIOLETTE
Call him Horatio, Horatio Smith.

HOWARD
'Oh, good Horatio'? Yes, I like that, Hamlet's friend. (She puts her arms around him) And we must champion Oxford in this film. We should have stood up to Hitler's lies long ago. Same here. After all, a lie is a lie.

EXT. DAY EIFFEL TOWER
Howard and Violette standing in front, same place from where Hitler will be filmed on his day in Paris

Scene 42 - At the Churchill home, morning - winter 1940

Winston Churchill is talking with his wife about his recent meeting with Howard during which he encouraged him not to use the Shakespeare/Oxford story in the film he is going to make.

CHURCHILL
Leslie's a great actor. But this idea, to bring up this Shakespeare thing now, in the midst of a fight for all our lives ... well, I just don't understand why.

CLEMENTINE
Does it matter? If he adds some lines, who cares?

CHURCHILL
It's more important than that, you should know that.

CLEMENTINE

I mean, saying that Oxford was the author would just mean
that Hamlet was the author. Hamlet was Shakespeare. How
fascinating!

CHURCHILL

Yes. But then you move right on to Gertrude just might be
Queen Elizabeth, not to mention Lady MacBeth! No, no, no.
This is not just about art, it's about policy. Some secrets
should remain secret.

CLEMENTINE

Especially in the middle of a war.

CHURCHILL

Yes, yes. Maybe you could talk with him about this, at a
dinner party or something.? Just emphasize how we can't be
doing this now. Don't get into anything more than that, just
emphasize "not now." Try to get Maugham there, if you can.
Howard played him in *Of Human Bondage*, and they're good
friends. Somerset is someone who understands the larger
picture.

CLEMENTINE

Well yes, if you really think it's that important.

CHURCHILL

I do.

**Scene 43 - A dinner party at the home of a friend of Clementine,
April 2, 1940.**

*Present are: Leslie Howard, Clementine Churchill, Harold Nicolson,
Secretary, Ministry of Information, in his mid 50s, Kenneth Clark,
newly appointed head of the Ministry's Films Division (late 30s), and
Somerset Maugham, the world-famous writer now in his early 60s.*

HOWARD

Every American I've talked to has an unqualified
determination to keep out of the war. They condemn Hilter

but they are wary of us, many have the nagging impression that we British are "too clever by half."

CLARK

I fear for most Americans we're a lost cause already.

NICOLSON

And the crux of the matter is America. How far will she go, in view of our situation.

HOWARD

The world, and particularly the United States, must know not only how we fight but what we are fighting for --- and that we are determined never to give in.

MAUGHAM

Leslie, you're the most American Englishman we've got who's still truly an Englishman. (In the distance we hear the sound of air raid sirens. No one reacts to them.) Yours would be an ideal voice to speak to them.

CLARK

What about the English people who remain in the United States?

HOWARD

They say they can do more good work there, in Hollywood.

CLEMENTINE

But what about people like Aldous Huxley, Auden and Isherwood? Why have they absented themselves?

CLARK

(Looking at Nicolson) Why don't you write an article in *The Spectator* attacking them?

NICOLSON

That will make me nothing but hated by them. Is that what you want? (Everyone laughs)

CLEMENTINE
(Turning to Howard) What about this new film of yours,
won't that be of some help?

HOWARD
I certainly hope so! It's going to be interesting. I've decided
to play someone who's partly the Professor in *Pygmalion*,
and that fop in *Scarlet Pimpernel*.

MAUGHAM
Really? Am I in there anywhere? (Everyone laughs)

HOWARD
Well, if you were you could be the one to say that
'Shakespeare was the Earl of Oxford.'

MAUGHAM
I would never say that. (Everyone laughs again)

CLEMENTINE
Well, Leslie, you do know that some of us —no, actually,
many of us— are concerned that you're going to bring this
Shakespeare business into this film. It's so controversial. We
just don't see why, especially now, in the middle of a war.

HOWARD
Well, people are out there right now discussing it, even in the
middle of a war. Were you aware of the article in last
month's *Scientific American* about the X-rays of the
Ashbourne portrait? Now there is scientific proof that under
the Shakespeare mask lies Oxford. And that matters.

CLEMENTINE
Still, discussing this in public upsets many people, especially
now.

HOWARD
This is precisely the time to say it, when we're most in fear
of losing everything forever. Jesus himself said, "The truth
shall set you free." Truth is Shakespeare's word for God. In

the end, it's all that really matters.

MAUGHAM
Jesus! Hamlet! Leslie, you do remember how those stories end, don't you?

HOWARD
I know, I know. But principles matter. The truth matters.

CLEMENTINE
But shouldn't we be projecting a united front?

HOWARD
Let the Germans do that. We are the front of a hundred different colors. That's what were fighting for.

CLEMENTINE
(Looks over at Maugham. He shrugs his shoulders) Still, at this point ...

HOWARD
Yes, it isn't really about plays or literature at all, is it? It's about religion and politics, and myths and history.

MAUGHAM
(Firmly) No, no, no, Leslie. This is about winning the war we're in right now, and using your talent to create some effective propaganda. It is not the time to trot out your pet theory about something that happened centuries ago.

HOWARD
No, it's important that we honor the truth.

MAUGHAM
Leslie, it's a mistake to do this now. Please don't.

HOWARD
I'll think about it.

MAUGHAM AND CLEMENTINE look at each other, exasperated.

Scene 44 - At the Churchill home, later that week, April 1940

CLEMENTINE
No, no, he is very set on doing this film his way. And that includes the Shakespeare story.

CHURCHILL
What did Maugham say to him?

CLEMENTINE
He tried to make him see that this is not the time for this, but Leslie would have none of it. He went on and on about the truth. He did say he'd think about it, but I think he was just putting us off.

CHURCHILL
Has he never heard that truth is surrounded by a bodyguard of lies? Well, there's still time. Maybe he won't do it. We'll see.

Scene 45 - London, May 1940

EXT. DAY LONDON AIRPORT
plane landing

INT. MORNING STOWE MARIES
Howard, with family, reading a newspaper with the headline,
"Chamberlain Steps Down, Churchill New Prime Minister," radio
playing, ANNOUNCER breaks in

ANNOUNCER
This bulletin has just been brought to us. Early this morning units of the German Army and Air Force began crossing the eastern frontiers of Belgium, Holland and Luxembourg. The battle for France has begun...

ANGLE ON HOWARD
as he drops the paper in shock

INT. DAY RADIO STUDIO

as Churchill speaks into microphone

> CHURCHILL
> I appeal to French honor and integrity in this hour of crisis
> and firmly believe that American aid will now be
> forthcoming to the Allies.

INT. NIGHT MOVIE THEATER
Howard and Violette, weeping openly, watch newsreels of Hitler
standing where they had stood in front of the Eiffel Tower

INT. DAY SAME ORNATE PARIS OFFICE

Marshal PETAIN speaking to REPORTERS while behind him stands
a GERMAN GENERAL

> PETAIN
> I have received Churchill's offer of union. It would be like
> fusion with a corpse.

MONTAGE
of Battle of Britain, submarine attacks, airiel combat,
burning buildings

Scene 46 - London, spring 1940

INT. DAY BBC STUDIO
Howard standing in front of microphone as "On Air" sign lights up

> HOWARD
> Most of you, I'm sure, will know what I mean when I speak
> of the curious elation which comes from sharing in a high
> and mysterious destiny.

MONTAGE
of AMERICAN FACES listening to radios

> HOWARD (Voice over)
> The destiny of Britain we cannot know for certain, but we
> can guess at it an pray for it, and work towards it as we find

ourselves singled out of all the nations of the world for the rare honor of fighting alone against the huge and ruthless forces of tyranny.

MONTAGE
of battle scenes as the weeks pass

> HOWARD (Voice over)
> The happiest peoples in the civilized world today are we few, we happy few, we band of brothers, fearlessly waging the good fight against terrorism, domination and lies.

Scene 47 - London, spring 1940

INT. AFTERNOON VIOLETTE'S FLAT
Violette serves tea as Doodie, Howard and Wink, in Navy uniform, are just settling in

> WINK
> I've been made Probationary, Temporary, Acting Sub-Lieutenant of the Royal Naval Volunteer Reserve.

> HOWARD
> Delightful promotion! (To Violette) Though I think the title sounds a trifle insecure.

> VIOLETTE
> What kept you?

> HOWARD
> We were stopped on the way in. Air raids.

> WINK
> Whenever we happen to be together we draw bombs like iron filings to a magnet.

> HOWARD
> It seems the Germans are determined to liquidate us.

                          DOODIE
Just us?

                          HOWARD
(Laughs) Oh, the list is long, I know. (To Violette) Do you
know I heard they even tried to kidnap Prince Edward as he
was escaping through Spain. Use him as ransom or some
nonsense. What won't they try?

                          VIOLETTE
After *Pimpernel Smith* they'll want to kidnap you.

                          WINK
Really?

                          HOWARD
We play them for fools.

                          VIOLETTE
There's one scene, so funny. This fat Nazi claims, (Doing
accent, as if she were in a little skit) "Shakespeare was a
German!"

                          HOWARD
(Entering into the easy, playful spirit of two people in love)
No!

                          VIOLETTE
Oh, yes, it is very clear. Shakespeare was German!

                          HOWARD
(With a smile) How upsetting! Still, you must admit the
English translations are remarkable! (All laugh, but the
reality of her father's love for this woman registers on Doodie
and she is hurt and jealous both for her mother and herself)

                          DOODIE
(The only weapon at hand) Does that mean you're bringing

up the Shakespeare thing?

HOWARD

(Glancing at Violette) We're speaking up for Oxford, if that's what you mean.

DOODIE

You know how angry that makes people.

HOWARD

Let them be angry, I'm the producer. (Strained silence)

VIOLETTE

(Trying to smooth things over) Which explains how I got my little part as the shop girl, but we still haven't found a leading lady. (To Doodie) Has the acting bug ever bit you?

DOODIE

(Chilly) I've developed an immunity. (Silence. Sound of gunfire some distance away)

HOWARD

What's that? (Putting down their cups, they go out on the terrace to look)

ANGLE ON A SPLENDID PANORAMA
of London and the Thames stretched out far below while fighter planes can be seen wheeling like specks in the sky, the crackle of machine guns can be heard

ANGLE ON HOWARD AND WINK

HOWARD

It looks strangely unreal, doesn't it?

WINK

Like a mock air fight in *Hell's Angels.*

ANGLE ON PLANES
like dots growing larger

ANGLE ON HOWARD, WINK, VIOLETTE AND DOODIE

> WINK
> They're coming our way.

> HOWARD
> I disagree, old boy. They're making for the city.

> WINK
> I can see three Heinkel 3s quite clearly.

> HOWARD
> No, no, Wink, Dorniers.

> DOODIE
> And those are Spitfires having at them.

ANGLE ON THE AIR FIGHT
A formation of German bombers round which British fighters angrily weave, one of the bombers falls away

> VIOLETTE
> Much as I hate to disagree with you, Leslie, I think they are coming this way. Oughtn't we to take cover?

> HOWARD
> Oh, not to worry, except our tea is getting a little cold.

ANGLE ON OVERVIEW OF TERRACE AND PANORAMA
as they return indoors and the sound of approaching bombers grows louder over the stillness of the scene, then the rushing sound of bombs descending, then exploding in the same pattern as in Howard's nightmares, the last one hitting their building

ANGLE ON THE STAIR WELL
as they rush madly towards the basement, the building shaking all around, plaster dust flying in the air, the deafening roar of the bombs upon them

ANGLE ON THEM UNDER THE STAIRS
in the sudden silence and stillness afterwards, Violette turns to bury
her face in Howard's chest

ANGLE ON DOODIE
as she stares at them, hurt and confused

EXT. EVENING
Violette's destroyed terrace, empty above a smoldering London, a few
Spitfires fly by

> CHURCHILL (Voice over)
> Never in the field of human conflict was so much owed by so
> many to so few...

Scene 48 - Pinewood Studios, London, winter 1941

INT. EVENING MOVIE STUDIO
a party to celebrate beginning Pimpernel Smith

ANGLE ON ALFRED CHENHALLS
a big cigar in his jovial face, his rotund frame sitting at the piano, as
he gayly plays . He looks somewhat like Churchill, which is his
intention.

> CHENHALLS
> ...flying to high in the sky is my idea of nothing to do, but I
> get a kick out of you.

ANGLE ON HOWARD
walking over with MARY MORRIS, a very pretty young woman, on
his arm

> HOWARD
> Mary, this is Alfred Chenhalls, he helps me keep track of the
> money. Very important man. (Nods) This is Mary Morris, my
> new leading lady.

> CHENHALLS
> (To Howard) Lucky you. (To Mary) They tell me you were
> in Hollywood.

MARY

Briefly, but they didn't know what to do with a girl who wore short hair, slacks and no make up.

CHENHALLS

They love glamor out there.

MARY

And I look like Clark Gable, and then when they plucked my eyebrows I looked like a boiled egg! (They laugh) It's my forehead. I hate having my hair pulled off my forehead - it's such a big one.

HOWARD

Never mind. Mine's awfully big too - and do you know, I've done all right. (He smiles and she smiles back)

ANGLE ON CHENHALLS
watching them both with a twinkle in his eye

ANGLE ON VIOLETTE
as she comes over

VIOLETTE

Oh, Mary, congratulations.

ANGLE ON MARY

MARY

Thank you.

VIOLETTE

Oh, and the housing problem is impossible in London, it's much simpler if you just sleep at the studio during filming. I can set up a cot in Leslie's dressing room. (To Howard) But Leslie, 250 pounds is ridiculous. You can't pay your leading lady that.

CHENHALLS

Yes, Leslie, she must have at least 500.

ANGLE ON HOWARD
with a shrug

> HOWARD
> Then 500 it is.

> MARY
> Whatever you say. I'm thrilled just to be playing opposite you.

> HOWARD
> Thank you, my dear.

ANGLE ON CHENHALLS AND VIOLETTE
as he glances at her reaction

Scene 49 - Pinewood Studios, winter 1941

INT. NIGHT HOWARD'S DRESSING ROOM
Violette is setting up a bed for Mary

> MARY
> I thought when I missed my first appointment with him I was done for.

> VIOLETTE
> Oh, Leslie hates getting up in the morning too.

> MARY
> They told me he wasn't the fastest person out of bed...but also that he's one of the most sympathetic men in the business.

> VIOLETTE
> He is. (Pause) I'm afraid this will have to do. We'll be right next door.

> MARY
> Thank you, Violette. You are very kind.

INT. MORNING HOWARD'S BEDROOM
cold and dark as Mary creeps through, scarcely daring to breath

MARY'S POV
Howard and Violette asleep in bed, outside the window a full moon,
the room so still it seems like a dream

ANGLE ON MARY
sighing softly at the peaceful scene

INT. HOWARD'S OFFICE
Violette and Howard talking with Chenhalls

> HOWARD
> You think it's going to affect our box office?

> CHENHALLS
> No, no, but why bring it up? Who cares?

> VIOLETTE
> Leslie cares.

> CHENHALLS
> Yes, of course, but do you see anybody else sticking their
> neck out over this? Why make waves?

> HOWARD
> (Mocking) Ah, yes, Britannia waves the rules. (Suddenly
> serious) The Oxford stuff stays in, Alfred, and that's final.

INT. DAY. MOVIE SET
a JOURNALIST approaches Mary

> JOURNALIST
> Hello, I've got a petition here about Michael Redgrave. You
> know, the BBC is down on him for endorsing pacifist views,
> they're saying they're not going to let him work. It's
> frightfully unfair.

> MARY
> Well, I'm not very political but I don't think any actor should
> be stopped from working because of his beliefs. I mean, this
> is England. (She signs)

JOURNALIST
What about Mr. Howard?

JOURNALIST'S POV
of Howard fussing with some lights across the set

MARY
Let me talk to him.

JOURNALIST'S POV
as she takes the petition over, works on Howard as he half listens,
preoccupied with the lights

ANGLE ON JOURNALIST

as she returns and hands him the petition

MARY
Took a bit of doing, but there you are.

JOURNALIST
Thanks. You're a love.

INT. STUDIO SET NEXT DAY
Howard looks up furiously from the newspaper

HOWARD
Why is my name on this? I don't want to be dragged into this!
(To Mary) Why did you push me into signing this thing.

MARY
(Suddenly angry herself) Oh, Leslie, you know you did what
you wanted to do, and that it was the right thing. We're
surrounded by a lot of people right here in England who
wouldn't mind if Hitler walked in tomorrow...

HOWARD
Oh, Hitler! Don't go dragging Hitler into this!

> MARY
>
> Well, that's what it's all about! Why are you even making this movie if it isn't so people can say what they want?

ANGLE ON HOWARD
stopped short

> HOWARD
>
> Oh, I suppose you're right. (To Chenhalls) After all, what's another controversy, more or less?

ANGLE ON CHENHALLS
shaking his head

INT. DAY MOVIE SET
in a cave Howard holds a skull up to his face and recites lines from Hamlet

> HOWARD
>
> "Alas, poor Yorick...tell my lady though she paints her face an inch thick it will come to this." (He turns to the fat Nazi) The Earl of Oxford wrote that.

ANGLE ON VIOLETTE AND CHENHALLS
her smiling, him frowning

Scene 50 - Pinewood Studios, winter 1941

INT. DAY MOVIE SET
big, empty space, dusky light filtering thru

ANGLE ON HOWARD
with Mary

> HOWARD
>
> Now you think I've abandoned you, when suddenly I appear, I've come back for you.

RUN THROUGH
studio deathly quiet as Howard puts on her coat, looks at her

> HOWARD
>
> Come. (He stands, still looking at her over her shoulder)

MARY
(Quietly) Leslie, you should kiss me now.

HOWARD
(A little surprised) Do you think so?

MARY
Yes. (He turns her slowly round and gives her a gentle loving little kiss)

LONG SHOT
of the two of them, silently being filmed, and then suddenly everyone in the studio applauding

ANGLE ON HOWARD
looking up from a slightly bent head

HOWARD
(Softly) Yes. (He smiles at Mary)

ANGLE ON VIOLETTE
watching, worried

Scene 51 - London, May 1941

EXT. NOON LONDON STREET
a few days later as Howard, newspaper under his arm, rings a doorbell

ANGLE ON MARY
as she opens her door, surprised

INT. MARY'S LIVING ROOM
as they enter

MARY
This is out of the blue.

HOWARD

Hum, yes...well, Hitler didn't walk in, but his deputy did. (To her puzzled look he indicates a newspaper headline about the flight of Rudolf Hess)

MARY

(Laughs) Oh, Rudolf Hess. Yes, isn't it strange?

HOWARD

Must be mad!

MARY

Well, all those Nazis are crazy. (Silence) Can I get you some tea?

INT. DAY MARY'S LIVING ROOM
as they sip tea

HOWARD

Remember that day at lunch, you taking me to task about my pills? Telling me how silly I was being...(Imitating himself, slightly offended) "Do you think I'm a hypochondriac?"

MARY

(Laughing) I really think you need to be teased more.

HOWARD

Hmmm...

MARY

That's such a wonderful sound. It could mean anything.

HOWARD

Hmmm....(Silence)

MARY

Leslie, is there something on your mind?

HOWARD

I don't know. (Silence) The saddest thing about acting is that it really is all for nothing...

MARY

Hmmm...

HOWARD

It's the most self-deceiving of trades. (Pause) In a fiction, in a
dream of passion we can force tears in our eyes, a broken
voice ... and all ... so ephemeral.

MARY

And yet so intensely believed at the time...

HOWARD

Has it ever happened to you...that you've fallen in love with
someone that you're working with?

MARY

Yes...once or twice, I suppose...(She looks at him)

HOWARD

It used to happen to me all the time. I'd fall into these
passionate affairs that lasted the run of the show. Consumed
by them. (He can not look at her) It seems quite silly now.
(Still he can not look at her) And you've been quite
wonderful...

MARY

(In the silence she understands) Leslie, I'm not hurt that
you're not in love with me....

HOWARD

A vain fear on my part, I know...

MARY

No, you're an easy man to love. (Touches him
tenderly on the cheek) You're already in love...

Scene 52 - Outside London, spring 1941

EXT. DAY COTTAGE
in the English country side, red roadster drives up

ANGLE ON HOWARD
showing Violette the cottage he has found for them

> HOWARD
> Like it? (She smiles and nods) It's ours. (He pulls her into his arms) Our home.

INT. NIGHT MOVIE THEATER
Howard and Violette watching Pimpernel Smith *premiere*

ANGLE ON SCREEN
as his name in script appears above the title
"A Leslie Howard Production"

ANGLE ON HOWARD
beaming with pride to Violette

SCREEN
Howard, holding a book, in a room with a big fat Nazi

> HOWARD
> "This proves conclusively that Shakespeare wasn't really Shakespeare at all ..."

> NAZI
> "No?"

> HOWARD
> "No, he was the Earl of Oxford. Now, you can't pretend the Earl of Oxford was a German, can you?"

> NAZI
> "No."

HOWARD

"There you are."

ANGLE ON HOWARD AND VIOLETTE
uncomfortable stirring around them, confused remarks

ANGLE ON SCREEN
scene concluding

HOWARD
"The Earl of Oxford was a very bright Elizabethan light, but this book will tell you he was a good deal more than that. Sure you wouldn't like to read it?" (Offers it to the Nazi, who declines)

ANGLE ON HOWARD AND VIOLETTE
More muttering, someone murmurs "Hear, hear!"

MAN
(Breaking in) You anti-Stratfordians are lesser breeds without the law!

ANGLE ON HOWARD AND VIOLETTE
taken aback at his intensity

ANGLE ON CHURCHILL AND HIS WIFE WATCHING THE SAME SCENE AT A PRIVATE SCREENING IN THEIR HOUSE
They look at the scene, then at each other; she looks shocked, he looks angry.

Scene 53 - London, spring 1941

EXT. NIGHT LONDON STREET
Howard and Violette walking with Chenhalls

CHENHALLS
I told you to leave that Oxford stuff out.

VIOLETTE
Why does this Shakespeare mystery arouse such violent

opposition?

CHENHALLS
You know, if the Church of England had saints one of them
would be Saint Shakespeare.

HOWARD
I suppose he is sort of our national Bible...

CHENHALLS
And the author our national hero, our David, practically our
Jesus. If he's just another prince who posed as everyman, so
what? It's a lovely myth. Why call it a hoax?

HOWARD
Because it is. It doesn't affect the big picture. Look, if Jesus
was brought down alive from the cross, it wouldn't affect the
truth of his ministry.

CHENHALLS
(Laughs) Not to you maybe, but try telling that to the Pope.

VIOLETTE
And if this Stratford hoax were to collapse, people might
begin wondering what other stories they've been told...

CHENHALLS
Leave it alone, Leslie, leave it alone. Get a reputation for too
much truth telling and no one will trust you.

VIOLETTE
(Quietly)...and no one will protect you.

Scene 54 - Berlin, spring 1941

INT. PRIVATE SCREENING ROOM
DR. JOSEPH GOEBBELS, Nazi Minister of Propaganda, and AIDE
watching the end of Pimpernel Smith *as Howard disappears from his*
Nazi guards in a swirl of fog, invisible but vowing, "I'll be back."

GOEBBELS
Another phoney savior. (To his aide) These Jews are very
clever, how they seduce the masses into bondage to their
self-sacrificing heros!

AIDE
Revolting.

GOEBBELS
But the masses are like a woman, they want a strong hand,
they want to be bamboozled. (Pause) Ban this film...and keep
me informed of Pimpernel Howard's movements.

Scene 55 - London, spring 1941

EXT. A STREET IN LONDON
outside a theater showing **Pimpernel Smith**. *We see John GIELGUD,*
Vivian LEIGH and Laurence OLIVIER

LEIGH
So what you think?

OLIVIER
About Shakespeare, I don't think he knows what he's talking
about.

GIELGUD
If you don't think it's Oxford, you've got a lot of explaining
to do.

OLIVIER
I don't have any explaining to do. (Gielgud and Leigh
exchange glances)

MORNING VIOLETTE'S COTTAGE
Howard and Violette at breakfast

HOWARD
I've been thinking of a film updating Hamlet to a Denmark

under the Nazi heel. I see parallels between Hamlet's time
and our own everywhere.

> VIOLETTE
>
> (Cautiously) Yes?

> HOWARD
>
> Think about it. Once again his country is on a war-footing,
> only now it is Hitler, not Fortinbras, who threatens invasion.
> Claudius has usurped the government, just like these
> Quisling-style collaborator regimes. And Hamlet is the
> embodiment of the national resistance, rising to rid the land
> of evil misrule. (He beams at her for approval)

> VIOLETTE
>
> And Oxford?

> HOWARD
>
> (Laughs) Oh, I'll leave him out of this one.

> VIOLETTE
>
> Still, do you think you can raise the money?

> HOWARD
>
> It'll be a hard sell, I know.

INT. DAY HOWARD'S OFFICE
he and Violette are talking to Chenhalls

> HOWARD
>
> I've found another script, not exactly Shakespeare, but pretty
> good, and I know we could find money and support for it
> right away.

> CHENHALLS
>
> Yes?

HOWARD
It's about the man who made the Spitfire.

VIOLETTE
(To Chenhalls) It's wonderful!

HOWARD
Poor bloke died '37, so he never lived to see the vindication
of his design or the final glory of his plane.

CHENHALLS
You're going to want to work with real Spitfires, aren't you?
In the middle of a war?

HOWARD
Of course. But I think Winston can help with that.

Scene 56 - Berlin, summer 1941

INT. NIGHT SCREENING ROOM
Goebbels viewing scene from The 49th Parallel *while an aide
whispers translation in his ear*

HOWARD (Off-screen)
"...they also believed in first terrorizing their opponent by
covering themselves in war paint and beating loudly on their
tribal drums. Well, doesn't that sound familiar to you?"

GERMAN CAPTAIN (Off-screen)
"Familiar? I don't quite understand."

ANGLE ON HOWARD
in movie

HOWARD
What price Goebbels, eh?

ANGLE ON GOEBBELS
furious

ANGLE ON HOWARD
as later in scene the Nazis tie him up in a Christ-like pose and burn his books and paintings before his eyes

ANGLE ON GOEBBELS
satisfied

ANGLE ON SCREEN
as Howard walks slowly and deliberately towards a cave from where the Nazi is shooting at him

> HOWARD
> (Counting off shots) 1...2...3...4....(Hit in arm) That's the lot. (He enters cave, sounds of punches) That's for Thomas Mann, that's for Mattise, that's for Picasso and that's for me.

ANGLE ON GOEBBELS
sneering

CLOSE-UP OF HOWARD

> HOWARD
> Well, he had a fair chance. One armed superman against one unarmed decadent democrat. I wonder how Dr. Goebbels will explain that?

ANGLE ON GOEBBELS
becoming livid

> GOEBBELS
> How much longer must we tolerate this nauseating flood of insult? Churchill is behind this, him and that kraal of Hebrews in London.

> AIDE
> Disgusting.

> GOEBBELS
> What a riddle these English are. In their brutality, deceitfulness and pious hypocrisy they really are the Jews

among the Aryans. No wonder they use a man like Howard to mouth their lies.

AIDE
The English don't consider a lie to be immoral.

GOEBBELS
And these Jews think they can bamboozle everyone while they steal, steal, steal. Well, a punishment will be dealt out to them which is barbaric, but which they fully deserve. Thank God, the war provides such opportunities. And as for Howard, if I had him in front of me, I'd shoot him.

Scene 57 - London, summer 1941

INT. DAY WINSTON CHURCHILL'S OFFICE. HOWARD AND EDEN ARE PRESENT.

HOWARD
What do you make of this Hess business? Did he really believe there are leaders in England willing   to sue for peace?

EDEN
(Laughs) He seemed to think the Duke of Hamilton could stop the war! The fanciful ignorance of these people.

HOWARD
I heard they even tried to kidnap Prince Edward --- in Spain. Some say that they were saying after they win the war they'd make him King!

ANGLE ON CHURCHILL
as he just shakes his head without replying

HOWARD
But what about Hess? Was he insane? How could he think anyone over here would deal with him?

CHURCHILL

Goebbels called him a "victim of hallucinations." Who can
say? Some sort of lone nut. The incident was as unexpected
and inexplicable to us as it was to them.

HOWARD

Surely he must have had some understanding with someone
before taking such a risk.

CHURCHILL

No, he was on his own. Trust me. (Pause) Now, anyway,
what about this Mitchell film? We need to be celebrating our
heroes right now, even as we fight. The Spitfire may just be
our salvation.

HOWARD

Yes, I want the public to learn something of this unassuming
fellow, working quietly in the background, with little credit
or congratulation, during that time when Britain drifted
blindly through appeasement. When nobody listened.

CHURCHILL

A story that needs telling.

HOWARD

We'll call it *First of the Few*. (Churchill cocks an
eye)

CHURCHILL

I'll write a letter requesting all possible facilities be accorded
your production.

HOWARD

Thank you.

EDEN

What else are you working on?

HOWARD

Did a small bit in a film about some Germans trying to

escape across Canada. You'll like that one. And I'm thinking of filming a Hamlet set in Denmark today.

CHURCHILL
Not going to trumpet that Shakespeare pretender again, are you?

HOWARD
Oh, no, no. Not now. (Pause) But I could get you a copy of a book about him. (Churchill holds up his hand in refusal)

CHURCHILL
No, don't. I do not care to have my myths tampered with.

HOWARD
It's such a ripping good tale, it really is! Shakespeare was a real Scarlet Pimpernel. Once this war is over I'm going to make a movie about Oxford. It is a story that must be told.

ANGLE ON CHURCHILL
as he considers Howard thoughtfully

EDEN
You'd be just the man to do it.

CHURCHILL
You know Leslie, myths do matter. Every culture has its mythic heros, and Shakespeare is now one of ours. It's not a good idea for anyone to go out and change that.

HOWARD
What about truth? Where does that fit in?

CHURCHILL
Myths tell a higher truth, you know that.

HOWARD
The true Shakespeare was a hero, and he deserves to be recognized and honored. And some day that's what I intend to do

CHURCHILL
(Looks at Howard thoughtfully for a moment, then looks over at Eden) Well, are we about done with our meeting? Any more questions?

EDEN
No, I think we've covered everything,

HOWARD
I'd better be off then. Lots to do.

THEY ALL SHAKE HANDS. HOWARD LEAVES

CHURCHILL
You know, this is a very troubling idea Leslie has, I mean, telling the world the truth about Shakespeare in a film. Not a good idea. There is too much to protect here ... the royal family, the Church, the state. No, not a good idea at all.

EDEN
I know. But, what are you going to do? If he wants to make a film, he'll make a film.

CHURCHILL
We can't let that happen.

EDEN
Really?

CHURCHILL
It's just not a good idea at all.

ANGLE ON EDEN
his face filled with agreement and fear.

EVENING IN WAR ROOM
Men listening to a broadcast by Lord Haw Haw, the British Nazi in Berlin

LORD HAW HAW
...and this sarcastic British actor, Leslie Howard, will be liquidated along with the rest of the "Churchill clique" after the German invasion.

FIRST MAN
Listen to what they're saying on the radio about Leslie Howard!

SECOND MAN
I know, I know. He'd better watch his back.

Scene 58 - Denham Studios / outside London, winter 1942

MONTAGE
of work on filming First of the Few on location

MONTAGE ENDS WITH CUT TO SHOT OF DAVID NIVEN AND MERLE OBERON TALKING.

OBERON
How do you like working with Leslie?

NIVEN
He's a fine fellow, but, you know, not always there, if you know what I mean. Thinking about something else even as we talk. Busy little brain, always going. Some people may think him naive, but he's about as naïve as General Motors.

OBERON
(Laughs) I know, I know. I still love him, you know. There's no one quite like Leslie.

They laugh together

INT. DAY MOVIE STUDIO
a set for Few *of an English cottage not unlike Violette's*

ANGLE ON
Howard, his new LEADING LADY, Violette, David Niven and an

154

upset CAMERAMAN

> **CAMERAMAN**
> She does not look pretty when she cries.

> **HOWARD**
> I know, I know. Look, this is our last scene. Let's just get it over with.

TWO SHOT
Howard and his leading lady

> **HOWARD**
> In film nothing matters but your eyes. Just concentrate on your feelings. (She nods)

INT. STUDIO HOWARD'S DEATH SCENE
reclining in a chair under a tree in his garden, he seems merely to fall asleep

ANGLE ON HIS LEADING LADY
crying very simple, very real tears

ANGLE ON VIOLETTE
watching sadly, full of wonder

EXT. NIGHT VIOLETTE'S COTTAGE
INT. NIGHT HER LIVING ROOM
Howard sitting with Violette, late at night, she looks troubled and melancholy

> **HOWARD**
> Now I'll have to start beating the drum in earnest for Hamlet. (She sighs and he puts his arm around her) Remember when we were in California, alone, before *Gone With The Wind*...

> **VIOLETTE**
> (Wistfully) Those days were the peak. We shall never have anything like that again.

HOWARD
Of course we will. We shall go back, we'll recapture them.

VIOLETTE
No...no...they are gone forever...

Scene 59 - London, summer 1942

INT. DAY BRITISH COUNCIL OFFICE
Howard with Jack Beddington

HOWARD
What I'm really looking for is support for this Hamlet project.

BEDDINGTON
I know but I don't think we can be of much help there,
sorry...but how'd you like to make a lecture tour, say to
Spain?

HOWARD
Spain? I'm really not the right person for that kind of thing.

BEDDINGTON
It's more important than you think. A European invasion is
still more than a year off. It's vital that Spain stay out of the
war. We need people like you to advance the Allied
viewpoint against the reams of propaganda Goebbels has
pouring out of Madrid.

HOWARD
I hear there's still tremendous anti-British feeling there and I
don't want to be a lightening rod for it. I'm famous for
despising Nazis. Why tempt fate?

BEDDINGTON
Well, give it some thought. (Pause) Could you make a public
appearance in London as Lord Nelson?

ANGLE ON HOWARD'S FACE
nodding wearily

EXT. DAY ST. PAUL'S CATHEDRAL LONDON
ANGLE ON HOWARD'S FACE
in Lord Nelson costume, preparing for his entrance

ANGLE ON ST. PAUL'S
in stillness he emerges from the Cathedral, a spare, almost ghostly figure in a silver-grey uniform

ANGLE ON HOWARD
as he kneels at the top of the steps, a hush comes over the crowd

ANGLE ON THE CROWD
a silent sea of English faces

ANGLE ON RUTH AND DOODIE
in privileged seats in front of the vast swell of onlookers

> HOWARD
> For myself individually I commit my life to Him who made me...

ANGLE ON VIOLETTE
glimpsed discreetly in the background

> HOWARD
> ...and may his blessing light upon my endeavors for serving my Country faithfully, to Him I resign myself and the Just cause which is entrusted to me to defend.

ANGLE ON HOWARD'S FACE
from below, the steeple and wide blue sky above, as if he might be back in that time, and then a squadron of RAF Spitfires fly silently into view behind him

> HOWARD
> Amen, amen, amen...

ANGLE ON VIOLETTE
looking at Howard lovingly.

Scene 60 - Outside London, fall 1942

INT. NIGHT VIOLETTE'S COTTAGE
Howard, Violette and Chenhalls finishing dinner around an oval
table, a log fire lit, curtains drawn

CHENHALLS
Leslie, you look worn out. Why not a trip into the sunshine,
some place like Portugal perhaps? I hear life in Lisbon goes
on almost as if there were no war, lots of food and drink. Or
even back to America? Just take some time off, relax a bit.

HOWARD
No. I've got too much to do. And in any event, travel is
getting more dangerous, especially for anyone our German
friends are watching. I've heard that Merle and some others
were wisked out of New York in the dead of night last
August by security because they feared what the Germans
might be up to.

CHENHALLS
I understand. But still, I could accompany you, and we could
make any trip profitable, promote the sale of our films and
other British products.

HOWARD
Well, perhaps. Someone from the British Council was trying
to interest me recently in going to Spain on a lecture tour,
good propaganda and all that. I told them no, but ....(Looks at
Violette)

VIOLETTE
(Adamant) No, no, no. It would be very wrong for you to
leave England. You're far too valuable on the home front.

HOWARD
I suppose.

VIOLETTE
There are others who can be spared for that kind of work.

> HOWARD
>
> Well, it's the holiday...

> VIOLETTE
>
> There's always a risk with a long journey over water.

ANGLE ON HOWARD
smiling with a defensive shrug at Chenhalls

> VIOLETTE
>
> (Not letting go) A plane has already been lost flying to Sweden.

> HOWARD
>
> I know...

> VIOLETTE
>
> Leslie, darling...

ANGLE ON HOWARD
looking at Chenhalls helplessly, then closing his eyes with weariness

INT. NIGHT VIOLETTE'S COTTAGE
Howard working at the table, then slowly lowering his head to rest it on the back of his hand

ANGLE ON VIOLETTE
as she lifts his face and feels his forehead

> VIOLETTE
>
> Leslie, get undressed and go to bed. I'll call the studio.

INT. NIGHT BEDROOM
Violette tucking Howard into bed

INT. NIGHT LIVING ROOM
Violette on phone

> VIOLETTE
>
> Leslie has a feverish cold, I'm keeping him home for a few

days.

INT. DAY LIVING ROOM
Howard, bundled in blankets, laying on the sofa, putting aside a
script, Violette standing over him with a steaming cup

HOWARD
I can't, head's too thick, eyes bleary.

VIOLETTE
(Sitting) Here, eat this.

HOWARD
(He studies her) You don't look too well either. You're tired.
What's that on your nose?

VIOLETTE
It's nothing, but it looks very unattractive.

HOWARD
(Reaching out to gingerly to touch it) It's not a boil, is it?
(She recoils at his touch, then laughs)

VIOLETTE
It's just a big ugly pimple. (Pause)

HOWARD
We're a fine pair. After the war things will be different. I
won't be a national symbol anymore, just another movie
mogul...with his beautiful young wife.

VIOLETTE
(Protesting) Leslie...

HOWARD
It's what I want, it's what I'll do.

INT. MORNING LIVING ROOM
a few days later, at breakfast Howard is feeling better but Violette,
in reaching for the milk, almost misses it

ANGLE ON HOWARD
concerned

> HOWARD
>
> Darling...

> VIOLETTE
>
> (Touching her nose) This thing...it's my vision, everything's double.

> HOWARD
>
> Darling, I'm calling the doctor.

INT. DAY BEDROOM DOCTOR
talking to Howard at door, Violette sleeping in background

> DOCTOR
>
> Give her two of these every four hours and we'll see what happens.

INT. NIGHT BEDROOM
Violette in bed, looking worse, NURSE standing nearby

> NURSE
>
> Leslie, I think we'd better take her to hospital.

INT. NIGHT LIVING ROOM
Howard on phone to Ruth

> HOWARD
>
> It's Violette, she's very ill. We're taking her to London.

ANGLE ON RUTH
at Stowe Maries

> RUTH
>
> Doodie and I will come down right away.

INT. DAY CAR
HOWARD'S POV

*ambulance traveling through fog shrouded but familiar, winding
roads*

ANGLE ON HOWARD
following in red roadster, hands clutching wheel

Scene 61 - Stepney, London, November 1942

EXT. DAY HOSPITAL
*ghastly, ugly red brick building, ambulance pulls up, followed closely
by roadster*

INT. DAY HOSPITAL ROOM
*Violette being wheeled into gloomy little room with a bomb proof
bricked up window, her eyes are covered*

> VIOLETTE
> It's quite a nice room...

ANGLE ON NURSES
as they smile at each other

INT. EVENING HOSPITAL ROOM
*Howard sits alone by her, his hand on her head, trying to give her
the will to live*

INT. NIGHT HOTEL SUITE SITTING ROOM
Howard greeting Ruth and Doodie

> RUTH
> How is she?

> HOWARD
> I don't know.

INT. MORNING HOSPITAL ROOM
Howard coming to her bedside, her eyes still bandaged

> VIOLETTE
> Leslie...

ANGLE ON HOWARD
as he turns to DOCTORS, searching their faces

ANGLE ON DOCTORS
as they nod and smile encouragingly

INT. DAY HOSPITAL ROOM
Howard is alone with her

> VIOLETTE
> (Very softly) You could have done better as Ashley.

> HOWARD
> (Seeing she is slightly delirious, gently) But he was such a watery sort...

> VIOLETTE
> You just didn't try. You could have played him as complicated, as Hamlet. In love with Scarlett, but also with his wife...his honor...knowing in his heart Scarlett was wrong for him...

> HOWARD
> I love you.

> VIOLETTE
> I know, darling...(She falls asleep)

Scene 62 - Hotel near the hospital, November 1942

INT. NIGHT HOTEL SUITE SITTING ROOM
Ruth and Doodie watch as Howard gets off the phone

> HOWARD
> She's sleeping more comfortably. They're hopeful...no news till morning. (Smiles) They expect her to sleep through the night. (Ruth smiles back hopefully, her eyes full of worry)

> RUTH
> You haven't slept properly in a week. Get undressed and let

me give you a sedative.

> HOWARD
> I mustn't sleep too long. The hospital may call.

> RUTH
> Not till morning, remember. Here, dear, let me help you. If
> they call I'll wake you immediately.

INT. NIGHT RUTH'S BEDROOM
Ruth lying awake on her bed, phone rings

INT. NIGHT HOSPITAL DESK MATRON
on phone

> MATRON
> Is this Mrs. Leslie Howard?

ANGLE ON RUTH

> RUTH
> Yes.

ANGLE ON MATRON

> MATRON
> I'm afraid I have bad news.

ANGLE ON RUTH
despair darkening her face

Scene 63 - Hotel near the hospital, November 4, 1942

INT. MORNING HOTEL SUITE SITTING ROOM
Howard wanders in, half-dazed, stops short

HOWARD'S POV
a concerned circle of faces staring up at him

CHENHALLS
(Rising, deeply distressed) You'd better go back and lie
down...

CLOSE-UP OF HOWARD'S FACE
the truth dawning

INT. AFTERNOON HOTEL SUITE
Howard, Ruth and Doodie in sitting room

HOWARD
Cerebral meningitis...these stupid doctors...and the nurses,
why weren't they there? What were they doing? Playing
cards?

RUTH
They did what they could.

HOWARD
Oh, it's all my fault anyway! My indecision...I drove her too
far, asked too much...

RUTH
Don't blame, Leslie. It's a tragedy, that's all.

ANGLE ON HOWARD
staring blankly at them as if they were strangers

HOWARD
You never understood my feelings for her anyway. (Silence)

RUTH
We'll have to start making arrangements for the funeral. Do
you have her parents address?

HOWARD
(Staring into what might have been) Yes.

RUTH
Of course she'll have to be buried in England.

HOWARD
(In a sudden pained burst) Oh, don't worry about it! Who
cares? Don't try to stage manage everything.

ANGLE ON RUTH
hurt, turning away

INT. EARLY EVENING HOTEL SUITE
Ruth, just pulling door shut on a sleeping Howard, meets the eyes of
an angry Doodie

RUTH
This is the first real tragedy in his life. Since the last war
things have been so easy and uncomplicated for him.

DOODIE
Because of you.

RUTH
All the same, the dark side has never been this near before.

DOODIE
Movie people! He's always been naive about women, a
romantic dreamer...and he's been terribly cruel to you.

RUTH
He's led a charmed life and I have been part of it.

DOODIE
Mother...

RUTH
He needs me...and I love him.

Scene 64 - London, several days later, November 1942

EXT. DAY HYDE PARK
Doodie and Howard walking

                           HOWARD

I never realized how selfless she had been, how constant,
how she worked for my comfort and happiness. But I asked
far too much of her and this was the result. (Doodie nods,
thinking all this could be said about her mother) Her life was
thrown away, sacrificed and for what? Film-making! I was
blind not see how run down she was. She never complained,
only thought of me and this stupid, goddamned movie. Well,
the hell with it all.

ANGLE ON HOWARD AND DOODIE
slumped together on a park bench

                           DOODIE
You need to rest and take care of yourself.

                           HOWARD
How can I think of myself at a time like this? She's the one
who needed the rest! I have only one duty now - to devote
myself to her.

ANGLE ON DOODIE
her eyes going wide with shock

                           HOWARD
It's my fault she's dead. I must communicate with her...my
spirit with her, that's the main thing now.

                           DOODIE
(Firmly) Violette died through no fault of yours, you are not
to blame.

                           HOWARD
(Pause) You never approved of my relationship with her, I
know...

                           DOODIE
(Sharply) Perhaps you should have made an end of your
marriage years ago...but you didn't want that.

ANGLE ON HOWARD
staring, hollow eyed

ANGLE ON DOODIE
watching him till a sudden wave of pity makes her reach out to touch his hand

> DOODIE
> Shall we go back? It's getting cold - and you look tired.

ANGLE ON THE TWO OF THEM
her arm linked through his, as they walk slowly back

Scene 65 - Outside London, November/December 1942

EXT. DAY CEMETERY
Howard and family and friends at grave side

INT. DAY STOWE MARIES
Howard in his room, staring out into the garden

ANGLE ON RUTH
at the door

> RUTH
> Leslie, darling, dinner?

> HOWARD
> Hmmm... (He does not move)

INT. DAY HOWARD'S ROOM
Howard at his desk, scribbling something on a piece of paper, then staring out at the garden with a new light in his eyes

INT. DAY STOWE MARIES
Ruth and Doodie at foot of stairs, Ruth staring up with a worried look on her face

> DOODIE
> He's trying to communicate with her.

EXT. DAY STOWE MARIES
Howard kissing a sad faced Ruth good-bye, driving off

EXT. DAY VIOLETTE'S COTTAGE
Howard driving up, getting out of car, staring up at the windows

> HOWARD (Voice over)
> Very quickly after you left me you took hold of my
> consciousness and aroused in me a sense beyond my
> physical senses, an inner sense of seeing, hearing,
> feeling...we can never, never part...

ANGLE ON HOWARD
walking through front door, looking around

> HOWARD (Voice over)
> You made me know you were still beside me, you made me
> know that in the house I was not alone...you made palpable
> your touch.

INT. DAY STOWE MARIES
Chenhalls with Ruth and Doodie in living room

> DOODIE
> He's haunted by her.

> RUTH
> He spends hours at his desk, composing messages to her and
> receiving...replies.

> CHENHALLS
> We've got to get him back to work, before he drowns in
> sorrow.

Scene 66 - Pinewood Studios, Dec. 1942/winter 1943

INT. DAY HOWARD'S OFFICE
Chenhalls and Howard

HOWARD
This nurses script has possibilities...but *One Pair Of Feet*?

CHENHALLS
Terrible title but you could fix it, would make an excellent recruitment film for nurses. And there's always the Hamlet project.

HOWARD
Yes...

CHENHALLS
And what about taking a trip somewhere, a real vacation of some sort.

HOWARD
Funny you should mention that again. Here, look at this (Hands him a letter). The British Council wants me to go on a lecture tour to Portugal and Spain. More propaganda! I have more than enough to do here, and it will be much more effective. A lecture is once, film is forever. I've already written them a polite no, but they won't let up about it.

CHENHALLS
A trip to Portugal? I've heard Estoril is nice in the spring. Why not take them up on it? It would really be more a vacation than a trip.

HOWARD
No, I doubt that. It would just be a lot more work. And some risk.

INT. DAY MOVIE STUDIO
*Howard on set for nurses film (*The Lamp Still Burns*), distracted, not all there*

ANGLE ON CHENHALLS
walking over with Jack Beddington

CHENHALLS
Hello, Leslie. You know Jack?

HOWARD
Of course, how are you?

BEDDINGTON
Pretty fine, old boy, good to see you again. Sorry to hear
about Violette.

HOWARD
Yes, of course, thank you.

BEDDINGTON
I know how that can be. (Pause) So how's the film coming
along?

HOWARD
On schedule, more or less. You should talk to the director,
I'm just producing.

BEDDINGTON
No, I'd like to talk to you. In fact, what do you say if we all
go to lunch?

Scene 67 - London, winter 1943

INT. DAY RESTAURANT
the three men at a table

BEDDINGTON
What's the stop date for the production?

HOWARD
(To Chenhalls) Ought we to tell him? Isn't he a spy from the
Ministry Of Information?

CHENHALLS
(Laughing) No, no.

HOWARD
(Turns back to Beddington) We hope, optimistically, to
complete production in May. Is that any help?

BEDDINGTON

Well, I was thinking about that lecture tour. I'm aware of the
letter you wrote to the Council, but still, is that your final
decision?

HOWARD

Oh, that! Well, I really had been thinking absolutely no when
I wrote that letter, but now? (Pauses) Why not? Maybe a
change of pace would be good for me. You're not the only
one suggesting I should go, as you may well know.

BEDDINGTON

You're an important person in all our efforts to win this war,
and I think this tour would help with that. I really do. This
will be a critical year in the war, a turning point I think. But
the policies of Spain and Portugal are critical. They both
continue to support Germany, and that must end, the sooner
the better. They need to hear this message from everyone,
especially someone like you.

ANGLE ON HOWARD
as he sighs and nods and knocks out his pipe

BEDDINGTON

(Continues) They love you there and we need a spearhead, a
quality name to fly the flag, as it were.

HOWARD

(To Chenhalls) To go or not to go? (He pauses and glances at
Chenhalls.) To bear the ills I have than fly to others that I
know not of.

BEDDINGTON

It's really very important that you go.

HOWARD

Let me think. I do have a contract to fulfill right here and
now. My business, God help me, is making pictures. I have
few talents in other directions. And I have plans for other
films as well.

BEDDINGTON

Such as?

HOWARD

(Suddenly really interested) Well, I want to film *Hamlet*.

BEDDINGTON

Yes, you told me.

HOWARD

(Seeing the glazed look in Beddington's eye) At any rate, I plan to make it my major production for 1943. (Silence)

BEDDINGTON

Hamlet's a loser, Leslie. He dies. We're going to live and win this war. It's bad propaganda material.

HOWARD

People die on both sides, you know. Besides, a loser like Hamlet is more interesting to me than ambassadorial trips to Spain. And I do have to get back to the set.

BEDDINGTON

Listen, Leslie, it's the propaganda angle in this trip that's the primary target for the Foreign Office. Surely you can spare a month for such a vital task? They need men like you.

HOWARD

(Rising and smiling) Well, perhaps...

BEDDINGTON

(Patting Howard's arm affectionately) Anyway, old boy, think on it, as the Bard would say.

Scene 68 - Outside London, winter 1943

INT. DAY STOWE MARIES
Howard and Chenhalls before a fire, a cold, rainy day

HOWARD

Lately I've been having a recurrent dream of my first train ride into California, even to the smell of orange blossoms.

CHENHALLS

The orange trees will soon be in blossom in Portugal. (Howard does not answer) If you like, I'd be happy to go with you, to deal with the business details and all that.

ANGLE ON HOWARD
as he studies Chenhalls round, smiling face

ANGLE ON RUTH
entering from kitchen

HOWARD

Well, if we traveled together it wouldn't be such a bad idea.

RUTH

It would be wonderful, a change of scenery. It would do you a world of good.

HOWARD

Hmmm....but only to Portugal. From what I hear the atmosphere in Madrid is bound to be hostile. We might both be putting ourselves at risk, there's always the chance, slight though it may be, of some idiot taking a shot at us.

CHENHALLS

(With a laugh) I'm sure the British Embassy will make sure we're only involved with the right sort of people. Anyhow, not to worry. I may not be bullet proof but I'm certainly the bigger target!

HOWARD

All right, all right. I'll go to Lisbon, but no further.

CHENHALLS

Provisional reservations on the civilian flight to Lisbon have already been made by the Foreign Office. And here's a letter

they gave me to give you about it. I think Anthony Eden
wants to talk with you.

                    HOWARD
Hmmm...

Scene 69 - London, winter 1943

INT. DAY EDEN'S OFFICE
ANGLE ON EDEN
behind his desk, speaking to Howard

                    HOWARD
I am now thinking that going to Portugal would be alright,
but my friends all say it's really inadvisable for me to visit
Spain. I'd only be exposing myself to unnecessary risks.

                    EDEN
I understand, but this mission has now become very
important for a number of reasons, reasons that go beyond
just propaganda. For one thing it's not only important to
influence Portugal, which is basically friendly, but doubly
important to influence Spain, which is not. They both are
continuing to support Germany with wolfram shipments, but
Franco also has some troops fighting with the Germans. Very
few, in fact. But it is support. And now there is some concern
that he may try to take Gibraltar.

                    HOWARD
Well now, that would be very bad, wouldn't it?

                    EDEN
Yes. We had been hoping that he was starting to see the light
about how this will end, so he needs to know right now how
very concerned we are about his true stance on neutrality.
There will be a post-war world, and he needs to start
considering whether he will have any friends in it.

                    HOWARD
Well, if you think an actor can make all that much difference.

But seriously, how will my giving lectures on *Hamlet* have
any meaningful influence on Prime Minister Salazar or
Franco?

EDEN

It's not only lectures that we want you to deliver. There are
some very personal messages we need communicated, one of
them from the Prime Minister himself to Franco. Now we
know that Franco's already a fan of yours, so meeting him
would be no big deal, so long as the right arrangements are
made..

HOWARD

Shouldn't our ambassador in Madrid be communicating such
things to a nation's leader?

EDEN

He's recently gotten on very bad terms with Franco, and
Franco now refuses to see him at all. Just one more headache
in a world of headaches.

HOWARD

Oh.

EDEN

So you can see how important this trip has now become for
all of us. And there are others you should try to meet, such as
the Countess von Podewils, who we know will listen to you.
And she may even have some things to tell you, we hope.
(Hands photo to Howard).

INSERT
picture of a beautiful young woman

EDEN

It would be quite a boon to us if she were able to reach
England soon. She smells defeat, she's ripe to fall and she
knows Berlin ... intimately.

ANGLE ON HOWARD

HOWARD

(Long pause) How can I refuse?

EDEN

Thank you.

HOWARD

But I'll have to delay my departure a few weeks. I know reservations have already been made...

EDEN

That can be taken care of. I'd like to have a private dinner with you before you leave anyway, to take care of some final details. (Shaking his hand) You're doing your country a great service.

HOWARD

Thank you. (Smiling) If it weren't for serving my country I wouldn't go on the stage at all. My last public appearance I was Lord Nelson.

EDEN

Lord Nelson! (Shaking his head) You know that movie about him, *That Hamilton Woman*? Winston loves that movie! One night he kept us waiting hours just so he could see that movie again. The strangest thing...

HOWARD

You know one of the reasons Churchill loves *That Hamilton Woman* so much is that he wrote some of it.

EDEN

(Genuinely surprised) Really? (Recovering) Shouldn't be telling tales out of school...

HOWARD

(Laughing) He asked Korda to insert a speech he had written, the one where Nelson warns the world against Napoleon's tyranny ... (smiles) ...the play's the thing...

ANGLE ON HOWARD
smiling knowingly

Scene 70 - London, April 19, 1943

EXT. DAY LONDON STREET
Howard sees a headline chalked on a news vendor's board:
"British Civil Air-Liner Attacked!"

INT. NIGHT RESTAURANT
Howard and Chenhalls at dinner

> HOWARD
> Did you hear about that air-liner being attacked?

> CHENHALLS
> Yes, over the Bay of Biscay, they say. (Looks at Howard)
> The plane landed safely in Lisbon. It couldn't have been very
> serious --- nobody got a scratch.

> HOWARD
> Wasn't that our plane?

> CHENHALLS
> Our plane! How could that be?

> HOWARD
> I mean wasn't it the KLM London to Lisbon run, same as us?

> CHENHALLS
> It was. (Laughs) Have some champagne. I don't think they
> were gunning for us, old boy!

Scene 71 - London, April 1943

INT. NIGHT EDEN'S HOME
Howard at a private dinner with Anthony Eden

EDEN

You'll be using Hamlet as your text?

HOWARD

Mainly seven soliloquizes that emphasize the then and now sense, that make him so contemporary with us. One speech in particular refers to an impending battle for a "little patch of land" that must be defended to the death. Two thousand Englishmen pitted against twenty thousand Spanish, all of whom die "for a plot whereon the numbers cannot try the cause, which is not tomb enough and continent to hide the slain...that for a fantasy and trick of fame go to their graves like beds." (Pause) I don't think the parallel to Gibraltar will be lost on them.

EDEN

Excellent!

HOWARD

Oddly enough, this speech was inspired by an actual battle we had with them during the Armada days.

EDEN

Really?

HOWARD

It's said to refer to the defense of some sand dunes near Ostend by Sir Francis Vere.

ANGLE ON EDEN
glancing up with concern

HOWARD

The soldier standing guard when Hamlet opens is named Francisco. And Francis had an equally famous brother named Horatio.

EDEN

Turning into a bit of a family affair, isn't it?

HOWARD
And they had a cousin named Edward De Vere, who wrote
plays. (Pause. Looks at Eden.)

EDEN
(Making light) We're not going there again, are we.

HOWARD
It's just amazing how everything fits together when you
know who wrote Hamlet.

EDEN
I don't think we have the time for this now, Leslie. I really
wish you would just drop it. And anyway, it's so far-fetched.
I mean how could such a secret be kept?

HOWARD
It hasn't been kept. It's simply being denied.

ANGLE ON EDEN
looking away, shaking his head

EDEN
Well, it's all very interesting.

HOWARD
Interesting? It's fascinating. There are dozens of amazing
coincidences. Hamlet was attacked by pirates when he was
crossing the Channel, when the King sent him to England to
be killed? (Pauses) Oh, which reminds me, were you aware
of the attack last week on the KLM flight to Lisbon? Did you
know that was the one Alfred and I were originally scheduled
on?

ANGLE ON EDEN
as he nods his understanding

EDEN
Really? Well, that attack was a fluke, I'm sure. One
agreement that has been honored these last three years is no

attacks on civilian airliners!

HOWARD

Still, it does give me pause, as I'm sure you can understand.
(Pauses). Well, anyway, (laughing) we defy augury. Now,
where was I? Oh yes, Oxford was attacked by pirates while
crossing the Channel to England. May have been the Queen's
lover was trying to kill him. There are so many links like
that, it's way past chance, it really is.

EDEN

(Quickly) Maybe they knew each. At any rate, it's not my
field. I leave that sort thing to the experts.

HOWARD

Well, I don't claim to be an expert but still ...such a unity of
proofs!

EDEN

Yes ... but, what does it matter anyway, as long as we've got
the plays?

HOWARD

But the plays mean far more than you think. The players, as
Hamlet observes, can not keep council, they tell all. (Laughs)

EDEN

(Eden stares at Howard, concern on his face.) Leslie, I think
you're starting to become Hamlet, if you don't mind my
saying so.

HOWARD

Really? How odd, because that's just how I've been feeling
lately. It's done wonders for my talks on Hamlet. It's as if
I've really come to understand him, where just a few years
ago, when I played him in New York, I didn't understand
anything.

EDEN

Well, this is all very interesting, but we do have some work to do here. (Takes out a folder full of papers). Let's go over some of the messages we need relayed to the people you'll be meeting.

ANGLE ON HOWARD AND EDEN
looking over a sheath of papers.

FADE OUT

Scene 72 - Outside London, April 1943

EXT. EARLY EVENING STOWE MARIES
Howard and Ruth standing by his little red roadster in the driveway

> HOWARD
> I wish I weren't even going. You know how I hate traveling.

> RUTH
> You'll feel better about the whole thing once you're there.

> HOWARD
> Yes, you're probably right.

ANGLE ON THEM BOTH
as they embrace briefly, almost like mother and son

> HOWARD
> I don't know why - but I have a queer feeling about this whole trip. Still, what the hell!

EXT. SUNSET ROAD
the roadster traveling over the familiar road

Scene 73 - Airport / travel / Lisbon, April 28/early May, 1943

INT. MORNING DC-3
Howard and Chenhalls taking their seats

ANGLE ON HOWARD

looking up to notice patched up pock marks on ceiling, signaling a
STEWARD

> HOWARD
>
> What's this!

> STEWARD
>
> War wounds.

> HOWARD
>
> Was this the plane that was in the news last week?

> STEWARD
>
> The same. Such a thing has never happened before on this
> run.

> HOWARD
>
> Would you happen to know if it was the flight out of London
> or the return flight from Lisbon?

> STEWARD
>
> It was out of London. April 19th. I'll never forget it.

ANGLE ON HOWARD
leaning across to Chenhalls

> HOWARD
>
> So that was the flight we were booked on!

ANGLE ON CHENHALLS
as his good natured laugh is drowned out by the roar of the engine
starting up

EXT. DAY RUNWAY
DC-3 taking off

INT. DAY DC-3
Chenhalls sleeping, steward comes up to Howard

STEWARD
Please report any planes you might see through the port-
holes.

ANGLE ON HOWARD
looking up from his note taking to stare out window

ANGLE ON VIEW OUT PORT-HOLE
wide, empty blue sky

DISSOLVE TO ARIAL POV
*of Lisbon airport, planes parked like toys, some Spanish, some
American, some with swastikas*

ANGLE ON HOWARD
looking out port-hole

EXT. DAY LISBON AIRPORT

DC-3 landing

INT. AFTERNOON HOTEL LOBBY
Howard at register, signing name with a flourish

INSERT CLOSE-UP
of signature, just like logo in his movie

INT. AFTERNOON HOTEL ROOM
*Howard looking from balcony at the beach and the broad sweep of
the open sea below*

INT. NIGHT PRESS RECEPTION
*Howard moving among groups of admirers, flash bulbs illuminating
glasses on well-laden buffet*

ANGLE ON HOWARD
looking tired but gracious

EXT. NIGHT LISBON
Howard and Chenhalls strolling down the main avenue of the

184

brilliantly lit city, a contrast to blacked-out London

> HOWARD (Voice over)
> I'm rather nervous to be lecturing at the National Theater on
> so sacrosanct a subject as Hamlet, which they are all very
> serious about, and about which I don't know much --- and
> have forgotten most.

INT. DAY STOWE MARIES
Doodie reading letter, smiling at his modesty

> HOWARD (Voice over)
> Unfortunately, it has been put about that I am the great
> English Shakespeare expert, which God knows I am not. I
> think I shall come clean and admit all.

INT. NIGHT NATIONAL THEATER
Howard on stage before a packed house, inspired performance

> HOWARD
> "Not a whit, we defy augury; there is special providence in
> the fall of a sparrow. If it be now, tis not to come; if it be not
> to come, it will be now; if it be not now, yet it will come - the
> readiness is all. Let be." (Silence) This touches on Hamlet's
> philosophy of necessity and fatalism - a man must be ready to
> act, at all times, whether he feels like it or not...

ANGLE ON AUDIENCE
smiling, nodding

ANGLE ON HOWARD
later in lecture, leaning forward, beautifully read

> HOWARD
> "O God, Horatio, what a wounded name, Things standing
> thus unknown, shall live behind me. It thou didst ever hold
> me in thy heart Absent thee from felicity awhile, And in this
> harsh world draw thy breath in pain, To tell my story. The
> rest is silence."

ANGLE ON AUDIENCE
standing to applaud at end of his lecture

EXT. NEXT MORNING BALCONY
Chenhalls reading from a newspaper

ANGLE ON HOWARD
smiles wanly, watching a young woman walking on the beach, then looks out over the wide sea, searching

CHENHALLS (Voice over)
"...we saw a new Hamlet, original and unmistakable, a Hamlet-Howard who gave us an unforgettable performance, in the profoundly poetic voice of Shakespeare, of the collective spirit of England."

EXT. DAY COUNTRYSIDE
a train rolling slowly thru an orange grove in bloom

ANGLE ON HOWARD AND CHENHALLS
sitting by open window

CHENHALLS
(Breathing deeply) What is that?

HOWARD
Orange blossoms.

Scene 74 - Madrid, May 1943

INT. DAY MADRID HOTEL ROOM
Howard and Chenhalls settling in

INT. NIGHT RITZ BAR
a number of Germans notice Howard and Chenhalls enter, glacial stares all around

ANGLE ON HOWARD AT BAR
orders drinks from BARTENDER

>   BARTENDER
> (Quietly) Have you heard? The Germans surrendered at
> Tunis! We took a quarter million prisoners, including the
> German general and his staff!

>   HOWARD
>   Well, we must drink to that!

ANGLE ON ROOM
conversation stops, heads turn

ANGLE ON HOWARD
grinning

ANGLE ON GERMANS
reacting with looks that could kill

ANGLE ON HOWARD
as he lifts his glass to them and nods

INT. NIGHT HOTEL ROOM
Howard unpacking, Chenhalls sitting on bed

>   HOWARD
> (Glances around) You know, Merle Oberon may meet us in
> Lisbon.

>   CHENHALLS
>   I say! Merle Oberon?

>   HOWARD
> I have word she's flying in on the Yankee Clipper at the end
> of the month. Probably on some kind of mission, just like us.
> It would be lovely to see her again. (He looks at his suit case)
> My God, somebody's been through my luggage!

>   CHENHALLS
>   You're not serious!

HOWARD

Look!

CHENHALLS

(After a brief inspection) You're right.

HOWARD

My God, welcome to fascism. And it only contains some
clothes and my lecture notes. (Holds them up)

CHENHALLS

(Laughs) Photos of that are probably on their way to Berlin
right now.

HOWARD

Imagine Goebbels trying to decipher "To be or not to be..."
for secret messages! What fun!

INT. DAY GOEBBELS OFFICE
as he looks over photos of Howard and Chenhalls in Madrid, tosses
them on his desk and glances up at aide

GOEBBELS

Don't touch him while he's on Spanish soil.

INT. NIGHT HOTEL ROOM
Howard tossing in bed, suddenly waking out of a nightmare, looking
around in the stillness
INT. MORNING HOTEL DINING ROOM
Howard and Chenhalls at breakfast

HOWARD

I've been having one of my recurrent dreams. A bad one.
Ever since we arrived in Spain.

CHENHALLS

A recurrent dream?

HOWARD

Someone has a message for me...a dead person is trying to

tell me something important and I cannot understand what it is.

Scene 75 - Madrid, May 1943

INT. EVENING CORK CLUB
Howard and Chenhalls, at a reception, speaking with DR WALTER
STARKIE, a British official

> STARKIE
> The German Embassy has suggested that the next Allied moves will be against Spain. The police are treating British subjects as if they were conspirators engaged in plots...

> HOWARD
> And I don't even have diplomatic immunity.

ANGLE ON W.B. ISRAEL IN CROWD - STARKIE'S POV
ANGLE ON STARKIE
as they walk towards him

> STARKIE
> Leslie, I'd like you to meet someone. He's been traveling in Spain and Portugal on behalf of the Jewish Refugee Mission, been in and out of Germany many times now, actively plotting the escape of Jewish refugees from the Nazis.

ANGLE ON ISRAEL
smiling in greeting

> STARKIE
> Leslie Howard, W.B. Israel

> HOWARD
> How do you do.

> ISRAEL
> Mr. Howard! What a pleasure to meet you. How much I have enjoyed your films, and that last one, *Pimpernel Smith.* Delightful!

HOWARD
You are too kind. I only played the role. I'm told you have
lived it.

ISRAEL
We all have our roles to play.

ANGLE ON HOWARD
smiling

HOWARD
I understand you are trying to get some people out of Spain.

ISRAEL
Yes, to Palestine. But the Germans are very suspicious. They
think we have important people hiding under assumed
identities, so they make things very difficult.

HOWARD
But you don't?

ANGLE ON THEM BOTH
as they exchange a knowing glance and a laugh

ISRAEL
Oh, never, never.

Scene 76 - Madrid, May 1943

INT. EVENING DINING ROOM
as Howard and company take their seats at a large round table set
with silver goblets and trophies

ANGEL ON HOWARD
glancing around, suddenly gets up

HOWARD
There are thirteen people at this table.

ISRAEL
(Counting) Why, so there are.

> HOWARD
> (To Starkie) I'm sorry, I don't mean to be difficult. (He remains standing)

> STARKIE
> That's alright, Leslie. Not to worry. I'll have the Parson join us.

ANGLE ON STARKIE
as he beckons to a PARSON to join them

> HOWARD
> (To Israel as he sits, troubled) I'm not normally so superstitious...but I guess now I am.

INT. MORNING RITZ BARBER SHOP
Howard entering

ANGLE ON THE COUNTESS VON PODEWILS
the beautiful young woman in Eden's photo, watching him from the door of the adjacent beauty parlour

ANGLE ON HOWARD
as he sits in the chair

ANGLE ON COUNTESS
as she takes in the subtle effect his charisma has on the people around him

ANGLE ON HOWARD
as he notices her

ANGLE ON COUNTESS
as she smiles back

Scene 77 - Madrid, May 1943, party

INT. NIGHT BRITISH INSTITUTE
Flamenco party, a distinguished gathering including the DUKE OF ALBA, Spanish Ambassador in London, many ARTISTS,

THEATRICAL and LITERARY PEOPLE

ANGLE ON COUNTESS
searching room

ANGLE ON HOWARD - COUNTESS'S POV
as he makes his way through the crowd, his mystical quality seems to
have an evocative impact on men and women
CLOSE-UP ON HOWARD
as he greets Starkie and Chenhalls

ANGLE ON THE COUNTESS
as she makes her way towards Howard

ANGLE ON STARKIE
spotting her

> STARKIE
> Good Lord! What's she doing here?

> HOWARD
> Who's that?

> STARKIE
> Her. The Countess. She can't have been on the official guest
> list. She's the wife of a German officer.

> CHENHALLS
> Lucky Hun.

> STARKIE
> It's not good for you to be seen with her.

> HOWARD
> (Smiling) Oh, I'm a big boy now.

INT. NIGHT SAME PARTY
Howard and the Countess are sipping cocktails

                    COUNTESS
        Are you enjoying your stay in Spain?

                    HOWARD
        (Slight pause) Charming country.

                    COUNTESS
        But not so charming as England?

                    HOWARD
        Home, you know.

                    COUNTESS
        I've heard so much about it. I would like very much to visit
        your country...someday.

                    HOWARD
        We could discuss it.

                    COUNTESS
        I would like that very much. Perhaps a quiet dinner?

                    HOWARD
        Where we could go into detail.

ANGLE ON STARKIE
walking towards them

                    STARKIE
        Excuse me. Leslie, I have someone you really must meet.
        You'll excuse us?

                    COUNTESS
        Of course.

ANGLE ON HOWARD AND STARKIE
as the walk away

STARKIE
Leslie, do you know who that is?

HOWARD
(Curtly) I know precisely who that is.

ANGLE ON STARKIE
as he stops and looks at Howard

Scene 78 - Madrid, May 1943, same party

EXT. TERRACE SAME PARTY
Howard and the Countess

HOWARD
I'm using my Hamlet lectures to make points about the war
situation.

COUNTESS
About Gibraltar, you mean? I know, it's made them furious in
Berlin. God, how they'd love to get Spain into this war.

HOWARD
Do they think I have a secret message encoded in "To be or
not to be..."

COUNTESS
They think everything. (Pause) They could make things very
difficult for me.

HOWARD
Are you a German national? You weren't born there.

COUNTESS
I'm Polish-French, the daughter of an Argentine farmer. But I
always loved th English. I loved anyone who even spoke
English. (She looks at him) Loved the movies. I wanted to in
the movies.

                           HOWARD
              You wanted to be an actress?

                          COUNTESS
              I thought everyone wanted to be an actress.

ANGLE ON HOWARD
laughing, seeing in her other woman he has loved

                           HOWARD
              Well, it's not all it's cracked up to be. That's why I got into
              producing.

                          COUNTESS
              Yes, you would want to be in charge. You are a natural
              aristocrat.

                           HOWARD
              (Smiling) At your service.

                          COUNTESS
              When I made it to America I went straight to Hollywood.
              (Shyly) But nothing much happened except I did play some
              extra parts.

                           HOWARD
              An extra? (He looks at her, searching his memory)

                          COUNTESS
              No...we never met.

ANGLE ON HOWARD
smiling kindly

                          COUNTESS
              And then this German Count came along touring America,
              glamorous as a movie star, and I fell in love. I was only
              twenty four and he was a distinguished gentleman. (Howard
              nods at the familiar story) We settled in Berlin and then the
              war came.

HOWARD

And there you met the Nazi "elite"?

COUNTESS

Yes, yes, it was very heady. It was like being in an
enormous movie. But they're a strange lot, to say the least.
Rudlolf Hess was the only one who was what the rest of
them wanted to be. Gallant Rudolf.

HOWARD

Mad Rudolf.

ANGLE ON COUNTESS
mildly offended

COUNTESS

Mad like Hamlet.

HOWARD

What do you mean? He wasn't hallucinating?

COUNTESS

Let's just say he loved England too, and he couldn't
understand why this war should be between England and
Germany when the Bolsheviks are the real enemy.

HOWARD

Is Hess one of the reasons you're turning?

COUNTESS

He had the right idea. He <u>was</u> like Hamlet.

HOWARD

Why do you say that? (Pause)

COUNTESS

This talk isn't wise. (Pause)

HOWARD

Hess like Hamlet, what a thought! Betrayed by his own, do

you mean?

COUNTESS

Yes, betrayed.

Scene 79 - Madrid, May 1943, same party

INT. NIGHT SAME PARTY
circle of GUESTS, seated, awaiting FLAMENCO DANCER to begin

ANGLE ON HOWARD
glancing at Countess

ANGLE ON COUNTESS
smiling back from across the room

ANGLE ON THE DANCER
as she makes a dramatic entrance and proceeds to moves slowly
around the room, looking directly into the faces of her audience

DANCER'S POV
the faces go by until she comes to Howard, pauses, continues to
stare, becomes transfixed

CLOSE-UP
of Howard's face as she sees the skull glowing inside his face, turning
his flesh transparent, suggesting in eerie reverse the vision Howard
had of Oxford's face burning thru Shakespeare's gray portrait

ANGLE ON DANCER
screaming and fleeing the room as guests turn to one another
wonderingly, amidst a general murmur

ANGLE ON THE COUNTESS
staring at Howard inquiringly

ANGLE ON HOWARD
shrugging back, mystified

INT. NIGHT ADJOINING ROOM

Starkie trying to talk to dancer as she cries and shakes her head

ANGLE ON HOWARD
standing in doorway, looking at them

ANGLE ON STARKIE
looking back with a nervous shrug

EXT. NIGHT MADRID PARK
Howard and Countess walking after dinner in the warm, soft evening air, full of peace and mystery

                    COUNTESS
She saw your skull?

                    HOWARD
So she says.

ANGLE ON COUNTESS
shivering

                    COUNTESS
Does that frighten you?

                    HOWARD
Death? (Long pause) I'm in love with a young woman who died...

ANGLE ON COUNTESS
reacting

ANGLE ON HOWARD
smiling

                    HOWARD
No, it's all right...she has made me know, beyond all doubt, that there is no death, that man, above all things, is a spirit...and the spirit, once created, is indestructible...

EXT. NIGHT MADRID STREET

Howard and Countess, walking back to hotel

> ### COUNTESS
> I must make my move soon. After Stalingrad they know they have lost. They will get even more desperate and crazy now.

> ### HOWARD
> (With a harsh laugh) More crazy? Did you know they even made an attempt to kidnap Prince Edward while he was in Spain? Such idiots! Or Rudolf Hess flying his looney "peace mission" to England. Clowns, one and all!

ANGLE ON COUNTESS
a flash of defensive anger in her eyes

> ### COUNTESS
> (With a sudden, scornful laugh) What Rudolf did was not the act of a mad man.

ANGLE ON HOWARD
startled

> ### HOWARD
> What do you mean?

> ### COUNTESS
> He was invited. Hitler knew. So did Churchill. For years now, Prince Edward has been negotiating secretly with the Nazis for a separate peace that would put him back on the throne. That's what the "kidnap" plot was all about. Churchill knew all along but let it go on to buy time. But your precious Prince is a traitor. Not that the English will ever admit it. Any bad news about the British Crown always gets hushed up. In Berlin they think Hess has already been murdered and replaced with a double. The poor fool.

ANGLE ON HOWARD'S FACE
stunned

Scene 80 - London, June 1 1943

INT. HEADQUARTERS FOR BRITISH INTELLIGENCE -
EARLY MORNING, JUNE 1, 1943
A JUNIOR OFFICER approaches a SENIOR OFFICER

J.O.
(Handing him a piece of paper) Sir, this has just been
decoded from German Air Force radio traffic. Orders have
been issued for German fighters stationed on the coast of
Spain to attack and destroy an unarmed civilian airliner that
will be returning to London from Lisbon this morning.
Scheduled to take that flight is Leslie Howard.

S.O.
<u>The</u> Leslie Howard?

J.O.
(Nodding) There's still time to warn him off the flight.

S.O.
So that the Germans might wonder how we knew. Can't let
them know we read their mail.

J.O.
(Softly) Exceptions have been made, sir.

S.O.
(After a moments consideration) They'll have to make this
decision upstairs.

Scene 81 - Lisbon, June 1, 1943

INT. MORNING LISBON HOTEL
Howard and Chenhalls having breakfast

ANGLE ON HOWARD
staring thoughtfully out window, turning to Chenhalls

HOWARD
You never approved of my putting that declaration for
Oxford in *Pimpernel Smith*, did you?

CHENHALLS
Well, given the prevailing attitude it did seem a bit reckless.
Why not just do an interview?

HOWARD
A film has more permanence. Besides, you never know what
a newspaper is going to print. Look how the Spanish papers
suppressed my Hamlet lectures.

CHENHALLS
I'm sure Franco heard it. The right people always get the
point.

INT. NIGHT BRITISH INTELLIGENCE HEADQUARTERS
ANGLE ON JUNIOR AND SENIOR OFFICER

S.O.
(Looking up from orders grimly) Let the plane go down.
(They are silent for a moment)

J.O.
My God, all those innocent people ...I don't understand. If
the Germans want him that bad what the hell is he doing out
there?

Scene 82 - Lisbon Airport, June 1, 1943

EXT. MORNING PANORAMA OF LISBON SKYLINE
Cut to a group of people waiting to board a DC-3 at the Lisbon
airport, including Howard and Chenhalls

ANGLE ON A GERMAN MECHANIC
standing at the next hanger over, the Nazi flag flying behind him,
staring impassively

MECHANIC'S POV

of the little, laughing group standing by the gate

ANGLE ON GERMAN
watching them all laugh, unamused as the signal is given to begin boarding the plane

INT. DC-3
Howard and Chenhalls are settling into their seats

ANGLE ON W.B. ISRAEL
the last to board the plane, coming down the aisle, seeing Howard

> ISRAEL
> Mr. Howard! How nice to be making this journey with you.

ANGLE ON HOWARD
looking up with a smile

> HOWARD
> Mr. Israel! How good to see you again. Did things go well in Spain?

> ISRAEL
> Never as well as one would hope.

ANGLE ON STEWARD
at head of aisle

> STEWARD
> Pardon, but I must ask everyone take their seats.

ANGLE ON ISRAEL HOWARD'S POV
as he eases into his seat

ANGLE ON PLANE ENGINE
as it suddenly starts to roar

ANGLE ON HOWARD
glancing out his window

HOWARD'S POV
as the plane is beginning to taxi an OFFICIAL is running up to it,
there is a pounding at the door

ANGLE ON HOWARD
as a curious look crosses his face, the plane stops, the door is
opened, everyone turns to look and the official from the airport steps
on board

> OFFICIAL
> Pardon, is there a Father Holmes on board?

CLOSE UP - FATHER HOLMES

> HOLMES
> Yes?

ANGLE ON OFFICIAL

> OFFICIAL
> Reverend Father, if you please, there is an urgent call for
> you at our office.

> HOLMES
> Now?

> OFFICIAL
> If you please, Father, it is most important.

> HOLMES
> (After a moment, giving in with a shrug) If you say so, all
> right.

HOWARD'S POV
as he watches through the window while the priest is hurried away
thru the smokey wash of the prop like a man fleeing a storm

ANGLE ON HOWARD
a look of thoughtful concern on his face

EXT. VARIOUS ANGLES OF DC-3 TAKING OFF AND IN FLIGHT

INT. DAY DC-3
ANGLE ON HOWARD
suddenly being jostled about, his eyes springing open

HOWARD
(Momentarily frightened) My God!

CHENHALLS
(Patting his shoulder) Nothing, old boy. Just a little
turbulence.

HOWARD
(Settling down) You know, I think Churchill and Eden are
flying home from Casablanca today.

CHENHALLS
We should have hopped a ride with them.

HOWARD
Hmmm...

CHENHALLS
But I hear those transports are so noisy and drafty.

HOWARD
Yes, totally uncivilized.

INT. DAY DC-3
ANGLE ON HOWARD
staring out window

HOWARD
In a pamphlet that I've been reading it says that Edward De
Vere was actually the first son of Queen Elizabeth and then
they had an affair and produced the third Earl of
Southampton, who should've been the next king of England.

ANGLE ON CHENHALLS

>   CHENHALLS
> What?

>   HOWARD
> The first born of the first born...

>   CHENHALLS
> Now I know why Winston Churchill stays in Stratford.

(They both laugh. Long silence. Howard is lost in thought for a moment, then looks up as if he has just realized something that Churchill has undoubtedly known the whole time. Suddenly the sound of bullets ripping the fuselage, followed quickly by screams)

>   ISRAEL
> My God! We're being attacked!

>   CHENHALLS
> Why are they shooting at us!

ANGLE ON HOWARD
as he realizes why the plane is being attacked.

>   HOWARD
> (Whispers to himself) Me.

ANGLE ON DC-3 INT.
as cabin fills with smoke, screaming and choking, as the DC-3 falls towards the sea

EXT. DAY GERMAN PILOTS' POV
as burning plane crashes into the sea

INT. DAY BRITISH HEAD QUARTERS
JUNIOR OFFICER looking up from radio receiver

>   J.O.
> They got him.

Scene 83 - Berlin / London / Lisbon, a day later, June 1943

INT. DAY BERLIN OFFICE
a grinning Goebbels holding up a newspaper with the banner
headline: "Pimpernel Howard Has Made His Last Trip!"

CHURCHILL AND EDEN SEATED TOGETHER ON AN AIRLINER
ENROUTE TO ENGLAND.

> EDEN
> (Looks up from a newspaper he is reading) You know, that
> man Chenhalls traveling with Howard ... he looked a lot like
> you.

> CHURCHILL
> (Nods his head in agreement) That's it. They weren't trying
> to kill Howard, they were trying to kill me. (Eden looks
> away, shaking his head "no")

INT. DAY LISBON HOTEL LOBBY
Merle Oberon standing at desk where Howard stood, reading his
cheery entry, crying

INSERT CLOSE-UP
of his distinctive signature

Scene 84 - London, later in June 1943

DISSOLVE TO
GIELGUD and VIVIAN sitting at a restaurant.

> VIVIAN
> It's awful about Leslie Howard.

> GIELGUD
> I know.

> VIVIAN
> We're going to miss him so much. He was the perfect
> Englishman.

GEILGUD

A first generation Hungarian Jew ... our perfect Englishman.
He would have made the perfect Victor Laszlo in
Casablanca.

VIVIAN

Yes, would have. (Pause) After the war he wanted to make a
movie about Oxford.

GIELGUD

Really? (Long pause) You know, because of Leslie I was
starting to take all this Oxford as Shakespeare stuff more
seriously. I think he may have been right. But a movie? Not
now. (They look at each other.) Nor ever. (They both start to
laugh. They laugh and laugh.)

SLOW DISSOLVE
on the vast, tranquil sea as these words appear on screen:

In Memory of Raoul Wallenberg. After seeing Pimpernel Smith *he*
told his sister that someday he would like to emulate its hero. Of the
thousand he eventually rescued from the Holocaust most were the
Jews of Hungary.

FADE OUT:

THE END

Leslie Howard On Stage (1917-1943)

In London (a partial list)

June 1917. *The Tidings Brought to Mary (L'Annonce Faite a Marie)*, Paul Claudel. Strand Theatre. Actor: played Apprentice.

February 1918. *The Freaks*, Arthur Pinero. New Theatre. Actor: played Ronald.

July 1918. *The Title*, Arnold Bennett. Royalty Theatre. Actor: played John Culver.

January 1920. Mr *Pim Passes By*, A.A. Milne. New Theatre. Actor: played Brian Strange.

February 1920. *The Young Person in Pink*, Gertrude E. Jennings. Prince of Wales's Theatre. Actor: played Lord Stevenage.

July 1926. *The Way You Look At It*, Edward Wilbraham. Queen's Theatre. Actor: played Bobby Rendon.

August 1928. *Her Cardboard Lover*, Valerie Wyngate and P.G. Wodehouse, adapted from Jacques Deval. Lyric Theatre. Actor: played Andre Sallicel.

March 1929. *Berkeley Square*, John L. Balderston and J.C. Squire. Lyric Theatre. Producer, actor: played Peter Standish.

On Broadway, 1920-1936

November 1920. *Just Suppose*, A.E. Thomas. Henry Miller's Theatre. Actor: played Sir Calverton Shipley.

October 1921. *The Wren*, Booth Tarkington. Gaiety Theatre. Actor: played Roddy.

December 1921. *Danger*, Cosmo Hamilton. 39th Street Theatre. Actor: played Percy Sturgess.

March 1922. *The Truth About Blayds*, A.A. Milne. Booth Theatre. Actor: played Oliver Blayds-Conway.

August 1922. A *Serpent's Tooth*, Arthur Richman. Little Theatre. Actor: played Jerry Middleton.

November 1922. *The Romantic Age*, A.A. Milne. Comedy Theatre. Actor: played Gervase Mallory.

December 1922. *The Lady Cristilinda*, Monckton Hoffe. Broadhurst Theatre. Actor: played Martini.

February 1923. *Anything Might Happen,* Edgar Selwyn. Comedy Theatre. Actor: played Hal Turner.

May 1923. *Aren't We All,* Frederick Lonsdale. Gaiety Theatre. Actor: played Hon. William Tatham.

January 1924. *Outward Bound,* Sutton Vane. Ritz Theatre. Actor: played Henry.

August 1924. *The Werewolf,* Gladys Unger, from the play of the same name by Rudolf Lothar. 49th Street Theatre. Actor: played Paolo Moreira.

January 1925. *Shall We Join the Ladies?,* J.M. Barrie. Frohman Theatre. Actor: played Mr Preen.

January 1925. *Isabel,* Curt Goetz. Frohman Theatre. Actor: played Peter Graham. (Double Bill with *Shall We Join the Ladies?).*

Septembe 1925. *The Green Hat,* Michael Arlen. Broadhurst Theatre. Actor: played Napier Harpenden.

March 1927. *Her Cardboard Lover,* Valerie Wyngate and P.G. Wodehouse, adapted from Jacques Deval. Empire Theatre. Actor: played Andre Sallicel.

September 1927. *Murray Hill,* Leslie Howard. Bijou Theatre. Author, actor: played Wrigley.

October 1927. *Escape,* John Galsworthy. Booth Theatre. Actor: played Matt Denant.

September 1929. *Candlelight,* Siegfried Gayer with P.G. Wodehouse. Empire Theatre. Actor: played Joseph.

November 1929. *Berkeley Square,* John L. Balderston. Lyceum Theatre. Producer, director, actor: played Peter Standish.

August 1930. *Out of a Blue Sky,* Hans Chlumberg, translated by Leslie Howard. Booth Theatre. Director.

January 1932. *The Animal Kingdom,* Philip Barry. Broadhurst Theatre. Producer, actor: played Tom Collier.

March 1932. *We Are No Longer Children,* Leopold Marchant, book adapted by Ilka Chase and William B. Murray. Broadhurst Theatre. Director.

January 1935. *The Petrified Forest,* Robert E. Sherwood. Broadhurst Theatre. Producer, actor: played Alan Squier.

April 1936. *Elizabeth Sleeps Out,* Leslie Howard. Comedy Theatre. Author. (Originally seen as *Murray Hill* in 1927.)

November 1936. *Hamlet,* William Shakespeare. Imperial Theatre. Producer, director, actor: played Hamlet.

Leslie Howard on Film

Silent Films in England, 1917-1921

1914. *The Heroine of Mons.* England, Clarendon Company. Actor:
unnamed.
1917. *The Happy Warrior.* England, Harma Company. Actor: played
Rollo.
1919. *The Lackey and the Lady.* England, British Actors Company.
Actor: played Tony Dunciman.
1920. *Bookworms.* England, Minerva Films. Producer, actor: played
Richard.
1920. *The Bump.* England, Minerva Films. Producer.
1920. *£5 Reward.* England, Minerva Films. Producer, actor: played
Tony Marchmont.
1920. *Twice Two.* England, Minerva Films. Producer.
1920. *The Temporary Lady.* England, Minerva Films.
Producer.
1921. *Too Many Cooks.* England, Minerva Films. Producer.

In Hollywood and England, 1930-1943

1930. *Outward Bound.* Warner Brothers. Actor: played Tom
Prior.
1931. *Never the Twain Shall Meet.* MGM. Actor: played Dan
Pritchard.
1931. A *Free Soul.* MGM. Actor: played Dwight Winthrop.
1931. *Five and Ten.* MGM. Actor: played Berry Rhodes.
1931. *Devotion.* RKO. Actor: played David Trent.
1932. *Reserved for Ladies.* Paramount British. Actor: played
Max Tracey (first released in UK as *Service for Ladies)*
1932. *Smilin' Through.* MGM. Actor: played Sir John
Carteret.
1932. *The Animal Kingdom.* RKO. Actor: played Tom
Collier.
1933. *Secrets.* United Artists. Actor: played John Carlton.
1933. *Captured.* Warner Brothers. Actor: played Captain Fred
Allison.
1933. *Berkeley Square.* Fox. Actor: played Peter Standish.
1934. *Hollywood on Parade* (no. B-13)

1934. *Of Human Bondage.* RKO. Actor: played Philip Carey.

1934. *British Agent.* Warner Brothers. Actor: played Stephen Locke.

1934. *The Scarlet Pimpernel.* London Film Productions. Actor: played Sir Percy Blakeney.

1936. *The Lady is Willing.* Columbia. Actor: played Albert Latour

1936. *Breakdowns of 1936*

1936. *The Petrified Forest.* Warner Brothers. Actor: played Alan Squier.

1936. *Romeo and Juliet.* MGM. Actor: played Romeo.

1937. *It's Love I'm After.* Warner Brothers. Actor: played Basil Underwood.

1937. *Stand-In.* United Artists. Actor: played Atterbury Dodd.

1938. *Pygmalion.* MGM. Director; Actor: played Professor Henry Higgins.

1939. *Gone with the Wind.* MGM. Actor: played Ashley Wilkes.

1939. *Intermezzo: A Love Story.* United Artists. Associate Producer, actor: played Holger Brandt.

1940. *Common Heritage*

1941. *From the Four Corners.* Ministry of Information. Actor, presenter.

1941. *Pimpernel Smith.* British National Films. Producer, director, actor: played Professor Horatio Smith.

1941. *49th Parallel.* Ortus Films. Actor: played Philip Armstrong Scott.

1942. *In Which We Serve* (narrator)

1942. *The White Eagle*

1942. *Spitfire.* (first released in the UK by British Aviation Pictures as *The First of the Few*). Producer, director, actor: played R. J. Mitchell.

1943. *War in the Mediterranean*

1943. *The Gentle Sex.* Two Cities Films. Director, narrator.

1943. *The Lamp Still Burns.* Two Cities. Producer.

Selected Writing By Leslie Howard

Howard, Leslie, in Watts, Stephen: *Behind the Screen: How Films Are Made.* New York: Barker, 1938, p. 78+

Howard, Leslie. *Murray Hill: a comedy in three acts.* New York, Los Angeles, London : Samuel French, 1934.

Howard, Leslie, *Trivial Fond Records.* (ed. by Ronald Howard.) London: William Kimber & Co Ltd, 1982. (selections of Leslie's writings, edited by his son)

Howard, Leslie. "The Intimate Diary of an Opening Night." *The New Yorker*, October 31, 1925.

Howard, Leslie. "Such Is Fame." *The New Yorker*, November 14, 1925.

Howard, Leslie. "The Broadway Première." *Vanity Fair*, August 1926.

Howard, Leslie. "Stage Struck." *Vanity Fair*, January 1927.

Howard, Leslie. "Rip van Howard." *The New Yorker*, March 5, 1927.

Howard, Leslie. "Holy Hollywood." *The New Yorker*, May 14, 1927.

Howard, Leslie. "Poor Alice." *Vanity Fair*, July 1927.

Howard, Leslie. "Biography of an Anglo-American Child." *Vanity Fair*, September 1927.

Howard, Leslie. "Back-stage visitors: I – The Insurance Gentleman." *The New Yorker*, November 12, 1927.

Howard, Leslie. "Backstage Visitors: II – The Process server." *The New Yorker*, November 19, 1927.

Howard, Leslie. "Back Stage Visitors; III – My Public." *The New Yorker*, November 26, 1927.

Howard, Leslie. "One Man Theatre." *Vanity Fair*, January 1928.

Howard, Leslie. "One Happy Family." *Vanity Fair*, July 1930.

Howard, Leslie. "Doug Jr. As I Know Him." *Movie Mirror*, April 1934.

Howard, Leslie. "Romeo Talks!" *Film Weekly*, May 30, 1936.

Howard, Leslie. "Romeo." *Picturegoer's Supplement, Romeo and Juliet*, March 27, 1937.

Howard, Leslie. "Thespis – The Jade." *Stage*, July 1937.

Howard, Leslie. "How I Shall Play Lawrence." *Film Weekly*, November 20, 1937.

214

Works Cited and Bibliography

Adelman, Janet. *Suffocating Mothers (New York: Routledge, 1992)*
Agate, James, *A Short View of the English Stage, 1900-1926*
    (London: H. Jenkins, 1926).
Aldgate, Anthony and Jeffrey Richards, *Britain Can Take It: British*
    Cinema in the Second World War (Oxford: Blackwell, 1986).
Allen, David Rayvern, *Sir Aubrey: A Biography of* C. *Aubrey Smith,*
    England Cricketer, West End Actor, Hollywood Film Star
    (London:Elm Tree Books, 1982).
Allen, Percy. *The Life Story of Edward de Vere as "William*
    Shakespeare" (London: Cecil Palmer, 1932).
Anonymous, *British Security Coordination. The Secret History of*
    British Intelligence in the Americas 1940-1945 (London: St
    Ermin's, 1998).
Astor, Mary, *A Life on Film* (London: W.H. Allen, 1973).

Baigent, Michael; Leigh, Richard; Lincoln, Henry. *Holy Blood, Holy*
    Grail (London: Corgi, 1983).
Balcon, Michael, *Michael Balcon Presents . . . A Lifetime of Films*
    (London: Hutchinson, 1969).
Bankhead, Tallulah, *Tallulah: My Autobiography* (London:
    Gollancz, 1952).
Barnes, Elizabeth. *Incest and the literary imagination* (Gainesville:
    University press of Florida,2002)
Bartley, Anthony, *Smoke Tiails in the Sky: From the Journals of a*
    Fighter Pilot (London: Kimber,1984).
Beauclerk, Charles. *Shakespeare's Lost Kingdom* (New York: Grove
    Press, 2010).
Behlmer, Rudy (ed.), *Memo from David 0. Selznick* (New York:
    Viking Press, 1972).
Beider, Alexander, *A Dictionary of Jewish Surnames from the*
    Russian Empire (Teaneck, NJ: Avotaynu, 1993).
Beller, Stephen, *Vienna and the Jews 1867-1939. A Cultural History*
    (Cambridge: Cambridge University Press, 1989).
Bessie, Alvah, *Inquisition in Eden* (Berlin: Seven Seas Publishers,
    1967).
Blumberg, Sir Herbert Edward, *Britain's Sea Soldiers: A Record of*
    the Royal Marines During the War 1914-1919 (Devonport: Swiss,
    1927).

Boehrer, Bruce Thomas. *Monarchy and Incest in Renaissance England* (Philadelphia: University of Philadelphia Press, 1992)

Bolchover, Richard, *British Jewry and the Holocaust* (Cambridge: Cambridge University Press, 1993).

Breitman, Richard, *Official Secrets: What the Nazis Planned, What the British and Americans Knew* (London: Allen Lane The Penguin Press, 1999).

Breitman, Richard, *U.S. Intelligence and the Nazis* (Cambridge and New York: Cambridge University Press, 2005).

Brewer, Susan, *To Win the Peace: British Propaganda in the United States during World War II* (Ithaca, NY and London: Cornell University Press, 1997).

Brown, Frederick, *Zola: A Life* (London: Macmillan, 1996)

Brownlow, Kevin, *The Parade's Gone By* (London: Secker and Warburg, 1968),

Brownlow, Kevin, *David Lean: A Biography,* (London: Richard Cohen, 1996).

Brunel, Adrian, *Nice Work: The Story of Thirty Years in British Film Production* (London: Forbes Robertson, 1949).

Butler, Ewan, *Mason-Mac: The Life of Lieutenant-General Sir Noel Mason-Macfarlane: A Biography* (London: Macmillan, 1972).

Calder, Robert Willie. *The Life of W. Somerset Maugham*(New York: St. Martin's press, 1989)

Cave Brown, Anthony, *The Secret Servant: The Life of Sir Stewart Menzies, Head of Intelligence* (London: Michael. Joseph, 1988).

Cazenove, H., *Northamptonshire Yeomanry 1794-1964* (Northampton: Belmont Press, 1966).

Chandler, A.R., *Alleyn's: The Coeducational School* (Henley-on-Thames: Gresham Books in partnership with Alleyn's School, 1998).

Churchill, Winston. *The Hinge of Fate.* (Boston : Houghton Mifflin, 1950)

Clark, Kenneth, *The Other Half: A Self Portrait* (London: Hamish Hamilton, 1977).

Cline, Sally, *Radclyffe Hall: A Woman Called John* (London: J. Murray, 1997).

Cockin, Katherine, *Women and Theatre in the Age of Suffrage: The Pioneer Players* (Basingstoke: Macmillan, 2001).

Cohn, Michael, *Jewish Bridges: East to West* (Westport, CT and London: Praeger, 1996).

Coleman, Terry. *Olivier, The Authorised Biography* (Bloomsbury Publishing, 2005).

Colvin, Ian, *Flight 777* (London: Evans Brothers, 1957)

Constanduros, Mabel, *Shreds and Patches* (London: Lawson and Dunn, 1946).

Cooper, Diana, *The Light of Common* Day (London: Hart Davies, 1959).

Courtney, Marguerite, *Laurette* (New York: Atheneum, 1955).

Cull, Nicholas, *Selling War: The British Propaganda Campaign against American 'Neutrality' in World War II* (New York and Oxford: Oxford University Press, 1995).

Danischewsky, Monja, *Michael Balcon's 25 Years in Film* (London: World Film Productions, 1947).

Davies, Marion, *The Times We Had: Life with William Randolph Hearst* (London: Angus and Robertson, 1976).

Dean, Basil, *Seven Ages* (London: Hutchinson, 1973).

Dickens, Monica, *One Pair of Feet* (London: Michael Joseph, 1942).

Dickens, Monica, *An Open Book* (London: Book Club Associates and Heinemann, 1978).

Doherty, Edward, *The Rain Girl* (Philadelphia, PA: Macrae, 1930).

Drazin, Charles, *Korda: Britain's Only Movie Mogul* (London: Sidgwick and Jackson, 2002).

Duff Cooper, Alfred, *Old Men Forget: An Autobiography of Duff Cooper* (London: Hart-Davis 1957).

Dunkel, WB., *Sir Arthur Pinero: A Critical Biography With Letters* (Chicago, IL: The University of Chicago Press, 1941).

Eden, Anthony. *Facing the Dictators: the memories of Anthony Eden, Earl of Avon* (Boston: Houghton Mifflin, 1962)

Eforgan, Estel. *Leslie Howard, The Lost Actor* (London: Vallertine Mitchell, 2010).

Ellis, L.F., *The War in France and Flanders 1939-1940* (London: HMSO, 1953).

Emerson, Ralph Waldo. *Self-reliance and other essays* (New York

: Dover Publications, 1993) "Essays, 1841: History."

Emerson, Ralph Waldo. *Emerson: Select Essays and Poems.* (Boston, Chicago : Allen and Bacon, 1937). Essay: "Compensation."

Errington, Col. F.H.L., *The Inns of Court Officers Training* Corps *During the Great War* (London: Printing Craft, 1922).

Evans, Robert, *The Kid Stays in the Picture* (London: Faber and Faber, 2004).

Eyles, Allen, *Oscar Deutsch Entertains Our Nation: Odeon Cinemas* (London: Cinema Theatre Association, 2002).

Fairbanks Jnr, Douglas, *The Salad Days* (London: Collins 1988).

Fairbanks Jnr, Douglas, *A Hell of a War* (London: Robson, 1995).

Fishman, Jack. *My Darling Clementine, a story of Lady Churchill* (New York: David McKay Co. Inc. 1963)

Foot, M.R.D., *SOE: An Outline History of the Special Operation Executive 1940-1946* (London: Pimlico, 1999).

Foot, M.R.D. and J.M. Langley, *MI9* (London: Book Club Associates, 1979).

Frohlich, Elke, *Die Tagebuch von Joseph Goebbels* (Munich: K.G. Saur, 1993).

Gallagher, Tony, *The Adventures of Roberto Rossellini* (New York: Da Capo, 1998).

Gannon, F., *The British Press and Germany 1936-1939* (Oxford: Clarendon Press, 1971).

Gargan, William, *Why Me? An Autobiography* (New York: Doubleday, 1969).

Gifford, Dennis, *The British Film Catalogue,* 3rd edn (London: Fitzroy Dearborn, 2001).

Gilbert, Martin, *Winston S. Churchill, vol. 5, Prophet of Truth 1922-1939* (London: Heinemann, 1976).

Gilbert, Martin, *Winston Churchill: The Wilderness Years* (London: Macmillan, 1981).

Gilbert, Martin, *Winston S. Churchill,* vol. 7, *Road to Victory 19411945* (London: Heinemann, 1986).

Gilbert, Martin, *Second World War* (London: Weidenfeld and Nicolson, 1989).

Gilbert, Martin, *In Search of Churchill: A Historian's Journey* (London: Harper Collins, 1995).

Golden, John, *Stagestruck* (New York: S. French, 1930).

Gordon, Lois, *Nancy Cunard: Heiress, Muse, Political Idealist* (New York: Columbia University Press, 2007).

Goss, Chris, *Bloody Biscay* (Manchester: Crecy Publishing, 1997).

Gough-Yates, Kevin, *Michael Powell in Collaboration with Emeric Press-burger* (London: British Film Institute, 1971).

Gough Yates, Kevin, 'The European Film-Maker in Exile in Britain, 1933-1945' (PhD diss., Open University, 1990).

Gough-Yates, Kevin, *Somewhere in England: British Cinema and Exile* (London: I.B. Tauris, 2009).

Guiles, F.L., *Marion Davies: A Biography* (London: W.H. Allen, 1973).

Gulbenkian, Nubar, *Pantaraxia: The Autobiography of Nubar Gulbenkian* (London: Hutchinson, 1965).

Hadleigh, Boze, *Leading Ladies* (London: Robson Books, 1992).

Hamilton, Cosmo, *Unwritten History* (London: Hutchinson, 1924).

Hamilton, Cosmo, *Four Plays* (London: Hutchinson, 1925).

Harris, M.J. and D. Oppenheimer, *Into the Arms of Strangers: Stories of the Kindertransport* (London: Bloomsbury, 2000).

Harris, Warren G. *Clark Gable: A Biography*. (New York: Harmony, 2002).

Hayes, Helen, *On Reflection: An Autobiography* (London: W.H. Allen, 1969).

Hepburn, Katharine, *Me: Stories of My Life* (London: Viking, 1991).

Higham, Charles; Moseley, Roy. *Princess Merle: The Romantic Life of Merle Oberon*. (New York: Coward-McCann Inc., 1983).

Hillier, Bevis, *John Betjeman: New Fame New Love* (London: John Murray, 2002).

Hinsley, F.H. and C.A.G. Simkins, *British Intelligence in the Second World War, 5* vols (London: HMSO, 1970-90).

Holroyd, Michael, *Bernard Shaw: The Lure of Fantasy* (London: Chatto and Windus, 1991).

Hough, Richard. *Winston and Clementine, the triumphs and tragedies of the Churchills* (New York: Bantam books, 1991)

Houseman, John, *Run-Through: A Memoir* (New York: Simon and

Schuster, 1972).

Howard, Leslie, *Murray Hill: A Comedy in Three Acts* (London: S. French, 1934).

Howard, Leslie Ruth, *A Quite Remarkable Father* (London: Longmans, 1960).

Howard, Ronald, *In Search of My Father: A Portrait of Leslie Howard* (London: W. Kimber, 1981).

Howard, Ronald (ed.), *Trivial Fond Records* (London: W. Kimber, 1982).

Hyams, Joe. *Bogie: The Biography of Humphrey Bogart.* (New York: New American Library, 1966).

Israel, Lee, *Miss Tallulah Bankhead* (London: W.H. Allen, 1972).

James, Robert Rhodes. *Anthony Eden* (New York: McGraw Hill, 1987)

Johns, Philip, *Within Two Cloaks: Missions with SIS and* SOE (London: Kimber, 1979).

Kelly, Andrew, Richards, Jeffrey and Pepper, James, *Filming T.E. Lawrence: Korda's Lost Epics* (London: I.B. Tauris, 1997).

Keyishian, Harry, *Michael Arlen* (Boston: Twayne, 1975).

Knight, G. Wilson. *Shakespeare and Religion* (New York: Routledge and Kegan, 1967)

Kotsilibas-Davis, J. and Loy, Myrna, *Myrna Loy: Being and Becoming* (London: Bloomsbury, 1987).

Lasalle, Michael, *Complicated Women: Sex and Power in Pre-Code Hollywood* (New York: St Martin's Press, 2000).

Lawrence, T. E. *Seven Pillars of Wisdom.* (New York: G. H. Doran, 1926)

Lawrence, V and Hill, P., *200 Years of Peace and War: A History of the Northamptonshire Yeomanry* (London: Orman, 1994).

Leber, Annedore, *Conscience in Revolt: Sixty-four Stories of Resistance in Germany* (London: Vallentine Mitchell, 1957).

Leiter, Samuel L., *The Encyclopaedia of the New York Stage 1930-1940* (New York and London: Greenwood, 1989).

Lester, Elenore, *Wallenberg: The Man in the Iron Web* (Englewood Cliffs, NJ: Prentice-Hall, 1982).

Lillie, Beatrice, *Every Other Inch a Lady* (London: W.H. Allen, 1972).

Linnéa, Sharon, *Raoul Wallenberg: The Man Who Stopped Death.*

(Philadelphia : Jewish Publication Society, 1993).

Lipstadt, Deborah, Beyond Belief: *The American Press and the Coming of the Holocaust 1933-1945* (New York: Free Press, 1986).

Lockhart, Robert Bruce, *Friends, Foes and Foreigners* (London: Putnam, 1957).

London, Louise, *Whitehall and the Jews 1933-1948: British Immigration Policy, Jewish Refugees and the Holocaust* (Cambridge: Cambridge University Press, 2000).

Looney, Thomas. *"Shakespeare" Identified as Edward de Vere, 17th Earl Oxford* (London: Cecil Palmer, 1920).

Lord, Graham, *Niv: The Authorised Biography of David Niven* (London: Orion Media, 2003).

Low, Rachael, *The History of the British Film, 1906-1914* (London: George Allen and Unwin, 1973).

Low, Rachael, *Film Making in 1930s Britain* (London: George Allen and Unwin, and the British Film Institute, 1985).

Lumet, Sidney, *Making Movies* (London: Bloomsbury, 1995).

Macdonald, Bill, *The True Intrepid: Sir William Stephenson and the Unknown Agents* (Surrey, British Columbia: Timberholme Books,1998).

Macdonald, Kevin, *Emeric Pressburger: The Life and Death of a Screenwriter* (London: Faber and Faber, 1994).

McCabe, Richard A. *Incest, drama and nature's law, 1550 - 1700* (Great Britain: University press, 1993)

McFarlane, Brian, *An Autobiography of British Cinema as Told by the Filmmakers and Actors Who Made It* (London: Methuen, 1997).

Madsen, Axel, *The Sewing Circle* (London: Robson, 1996).

Manchester, William, *The Caged Lion: Winston Spencer Churchill, 1932-1940* (London: Michael Joseph, 1988).

Mangan, Richard (ed.), *Gielgud's Letters* (London: Weidenfeld and Nicolson, 2004).

Mason Brown, John, *The Worlds of Robert E. Sherwood, Mirror to His Times* (New York: Harper and Row, 1962).

Matthews, A.E., *Many: An Autobiography* (London: Hutchinson, 1952).

Meltzer, Albert, *I Couldn't Paint Golden Angels: Sixty Years of Common-place Life and Anarchist Agitation* (Edinburgh: AK Press, 1996).

Melville, Herman. *Billy Budd* (Chicago: University of Chicago Press, 1962)

Mitchell, Gordon, *R.J. Mitchell, Schooldays to Spitfire* (Stroud:

Tempus, 1986).

Montgomery Hyde, H., *Secret Intelligence Agent* (New York: St Martin's Press, 1982).

Morgan, William J., *Spies and Saboteurs* (London: Gollancz, 1955).

Morley, Sheridan. *John Gielgud: the Authorised Biography*, (New York: Simon & Schuster, 2002)

Neave, Airey, *Saturday at M/9* (London: Hodder and Stoughton, 1969).

Nicholson, Michael, *Raoul Wallenburg: The Swedish Diplomat Who Saved 100,000 Jews* (Watford: Exley, 1989).

Nicolson, Nigel (ed.), *Harold Nicolson: Diaries and Letters 1907-1964* (London: Weidenfeld and Nicolson, 2004).

Niven, David, *The Moon's a Balloon* (London: Hamish Hamilton, 1971).

Norwich, John Julius, *The Duff Cooper Diaries 1915-1951* (London: Weidenfeld and Nicolson, 2005).

Ogburn, Charlton. *The Mysterious William Shakespeare, the Myth and the Reality* (New York: Dodd & Mead, 1984).

Orczy, Baroness, *The Scarlet Pimpernel* (London: Greening, 1905).

Palmer, Lilli, *Change Lobsters and Dance: An Autobiography* (London: W.H. Allen, 1976).

Pascal, Valerie, *The Disciple and His Devil* (London: Joseph, 1971).

Persico, Joseph, *Piercing the Reich: The Penetration of Nazi Germany by OSS Agents during World War II* (London: M. Joseph, 1979).

Peterson, Theodore, *Magazines in the Twentieth Century* (Urbana, IL: University of Illinois Press, 1964).

Pincher, Chapman, *Their Trade Is Treachery* (London: Sidgwick and Jackson, 1981).

Pinero, Sir Arthur Wing, *The Freaks: An Idyll of Suburbia, In Three Acts* (London: William Heinemann, 1922).

Pound, Reginald, *Arnold Bennett: A Biography* (London: Heinemann, 1952).

Pritchard, Michael, *Sir Hubert von Herkomer and His Film-Making in Bushey 1912-*

Quayle, Anthony, *A Time to Speak* (London: Barrie and Jenkins, 1990).

Quillgan, Maureen. *Incest and agency in Elizabethan England*

222

(Philadelphia: University of Philadelphia press,2005)
Quirk, Lawrence J., *Claudette Colbert: An Illustrated Biography* (New York: Crown, 1985).

Read, Anthony and David Fisher, *Colonel Z: The Life and Times of a Master of Spies* (London: Hodder and Stoughton, 1984).
Reed, Nicholas, *Camille Pissarro at the Crystal Palace* (London: London Reference Books, 1987).
Rey-Ximena, Jose, *El Vuelo de Ibis: [The Flight of the Ibis] Leslie Howard* (Madrid: Facta Ediciones, 2008).
Richards, Jeffrey and Anthony Aldgate, *Best of British* (Oxford: Blackwell, 1983).
Rose, Norman, *Vansittart: Study of a Diplomat* (London: Heinemann, 1978).
Rosza, Miklos, *Double Life. The Autobiography of Miklos Rosza* (Tunbridge Wells: Midas Books, 1982).

Shell, Marc. *Elizabeth's glass* (Lincoln: University of Nebraska Press,1993)
Shell, Marc. *The end of kinship* (Stanford, Calif.: Stanford Univ. Press, 1988)
Schenkar, Joan, *Truly Wilde* (London: Virago, 2000).
Schonfield, Hugh J. *The Passover Plot: new light on the history of Jesus* (New York, Bantam, 1967).
Sebag Montefiore, Hugh, *Enigma: The Battle for the Code* (London: Weidenfeld and Nicolson, 2000).
Shepherd, Naomi, *Wilfred Israel: German Jewry's Secret Ambassador* (London: Weidenfeld and Nicolson, 1984).
Smith, Michael, *Foley: The Spy Who Saved 10,000 Jews* (London: Hodder and Stoughton, 1999).
Smith, R. Harris, *OSS: The Secret History of America's First Central Intelligence Agency* (Berkeley, CA: University of California Press, 1972).
Soames, Mary. *Clementine Churchill, the Biography of a marriage* (Boston: Houghton Miffin Co. 1979)
Stafford, David, *Roosevelt and Churchill: Men of Secrets* (London: Little, Brown, 1999).
Stafford, David, *Churchill and Secret Service* (London: Abacus, 2000).
Stevenson, William. *A Man Called Intrepid.* (New York : Harcourt Brace Jovanovich, 1976)
Stone, D., *Responses to Nazism in Britain, 1933-1939. Before War and the Holocaust* (Basingstoke: Palgrave Macmillan, 2003).
Stone, Glyn, *The Oldest Ally: Britain and the Portuguese Connection, 1936-1941* (London: Royal Historical Society, 1994).

Tabori, Paul, *Alexander Korda* (London: Oldbourne, 1959).

Tarkington, Booth, *The Wren: A Comedy in Three Acts* (New York: S. French, 1922).

Taylor, A.J.P., *Beaverbrook* (London: Hamish Hamilton, 1972).

Taylor, Mark. *Shakespeare's darker purpose: question of incest* (New York: AMS press, Inc. 1982)

Taylor, Philip M., *The Projection of Britain: British Overseas Publicity and Propaganda, 1919-1930* (Cambridge: Cambridge University Press, 1981).

Thorold, Anne (ed.), *The Letters of Lucien to Camille Pissarro, 1883-1903* (Cambridge: Cambridge University Press, 1993).

Thwaite, Ann, *A.A. Milne: His Life* (London: Faber and Faber, 1990).

Tomlinson, David, *Luckier than Most: An Autobiography* (London: Hodder and Stoughton, 1990).

Trewin, J. C. *Five and Eighty Hamlets.* (New York : New Amsterdam, 1989, ©1987)

Twain, Mark. *"Is Shakespeare Dead?" My Autobiography* (New York: Harper, 1909).

Vane, Sutton, *Outward Bound* (London: S. French, 1924).

Vizetelly, Ernest:Alfred, *With Zola in England: A Story of Exile* (Leipzig: B. Tauchnitz, 1899).

Walker, Alexander. *Vivien, The Life of Vivien Leigh*, Grove Press, 1987

Wasserstein, Bernard, *Britain and the Jews of Europe 1939-1945* (London and Oxford: Institute of Jewish Affairs and Clarendon Press, 1979).

Watts, Stephen (ed.), *Behind the Screen: How Films are Made* (London: A. Barker, 1938).

Wearing J.P. (ed.), *The Collected Letters of Sir Arthur Pinero* (Minneapolis, MN: University of Minnesota Press, 1974).

Wearing, J.P., *The London Stage, 1910-1939: A Calendar of Plays and Players,* 3 vols, (Metuchen, NJ and London: Scarecrow, 1990).

West, Nigel, *MI5: British Security Service Operations, 1909-1945* (London: The Bodley Head, 1981).

West, Nigel, *MI6: British Secret Intelligence Service Operations, 1909-1945* (London: Weidenfeld and Nicolson, 1983).

West, Nigel, *Unreliable Witness: Espionage Myths of the Second World War* (London: Grafton, 1984).

West, Nigel, *Secret War: The Story of SOE, Britain's Wartime*

Sabotage Organisation (London: Hodder and Stoughton, 1992).

Whitehouse, Arthur George, *The Fledgling* (London: Vane, 1965).

Whitman, Walt. *"November Boughs" The Complete Poetry and Prose of Walt Whitman* (New York: Pelligrini and Cudahy, 1948).

Whittemore, Hank. *The Monument* (Meadow Geese, Marshfield Hills, Mass. 2005).

Who's. Who in the Theatre (London: Pitman, 1912-81).

Wistrich, Robert, *The Jews of Vienna in the Age of Franz Joseph* (Oxford and New York: Published for the Littman Library by Oxford University Press, 1990).

Wright, Peter, *Spy Catcher* (New York: Dell, 1988).

Wyman, David. S., *The Abandonment of the Jews: America and the Holocaust 1941-1945* (New York: Pantheon Books, 1984).

Young, Kenneth (ed.), *The Diaries of Sir Robert Bruce Lockhart* (London: Macmillan, 1973-1980).

Name Index

Index to the essay "To Catch the Conscience of the King"

1) Historical Figures, Past and Present (Politics, Literature, Philosophy, Religion)

Batey, Mavis, 33
Bismark, 3
Blackmun, Chief Justice Henry, 3
Boleyn, Anne, 24
Bolingbroke, Henry (Prince Hal), 16
Bottomly, Gordon, 33
Cecil, George (modern descendant, Cecil family), 32
Cecil, Robert, 33
Cecil, William, Lord Burghley, 4,14,33
Cecil, William (modern descendant, Cecil family), 32
Charles, Prince of Wales, 10
DeGaulle, Charles, 3
De Vere, Edward, 2,3,4,5,10,13,14,20,22,25,26,27,28,29,33
Dickens, Charles, 3
Disraeli, 3
Eichmann, Adolph, 31
Elizabeth, Queen of England, 4,13,24,25,26,27
Goebbels, Joseph, 1,2,13,16
Greene, Robert, 14
Haw Haw, Lord (see Joyce, William)
Henry, King Henry VIII, 24
Hess, Rudolph, 5
Hitler, Adolph, 13,18,30
Holmes, Father, 21
James, Henry, 3
Jesus, 13,23,24,25,33
Joyce, William (Lord Haw Haw), 1
Luther, Martin, 24
Lyly, John, 14
Marlowe, Christopher, 5,14
Melville, Herman, 3,23,28
Mitchell, R.J., 16
Munday, Anthony, 14
Napoleon, 17
Nelson, Lord, 17

Peacham, Henry, 29
Quisling, Vidkun, 18
Seymour, Thomas, 26
Shakespeare, William, 1,2,5,6,7,8,14,23,24,25,26,28
Shaw, Lawrence, 10,16,27
Socrates, 23
Stacpoole, H. de Vere, 12,13,30
Stevens, Chief Justice John Paul, 3
Twain, Mark, 3,28
Vere, Francisco, 4,19,20
Vere, Hoaratio, 4,5
Virgin Mary, 25,26
Wallenberg, Raoul, 16,31
Watson, Thomas, 14
Whitman, Walt, 3,28

2) Contemporary critics, commentators, writers

Adelman, Janet, 25
Allen, Woody, 5
Anderson, John, 9
Anderson, Mark, 26,33
Brown, John Mason, 9
Colvin, Ian, 21
De Mille, Agnes, 8
Eforgan, Estel, 28,32
Elliot, T.S., 5
Emerson, Ralph Waldo, 23,24
Fitzgerald, F. Scott, 9
Freud, Sigmund, 3
Harrison, Rex, 30
Houston, John, 8
James, Robert Rhodes, 32
Joyce, James, 3
Keats, John, 14
Knight, G. Wilson, 23
Lean, David, 10
Lee, Sidney, 3
LeJeune, C.A., 1
Looney, John J., 3
Mitchell, Margaret, 30
Ogburn, Charlton, 26,32,33
Shaw, George Bernard, 10
Shearer, Norma, 8

Shell, Marc, 25
Stevenson, William, 22
Taylor, Mark, 25
Thalberg, Irving, 7
Thomson, Virgil, 8
Trewin, J.C., 24
Wilson, Dover, 19
Wilson, Earl, 30

3) Leslie Howard's family, friends and acquaintances

Asquith, Anthony, 11
Auden, W.H., 15,24
Bogart, Humphrey, 7
Chenhalls, Alfred, 19,21,22
Churchill, Clementine, 16,26,27
Churchill, Winston, 1,19,20,21,22,23,27
Clark, Kenneth, 15
Coward, Noel, 16
Cunningham, Violette, 12,15,17,18
Davis, Bette, 7
Eden, Anthony, 2,18,19,22,32
Gable, Clark, 30
Garnet, Tay, 29
Geilgud, John, 8
Houseman, John, 8
Howard, Doodie, 5,21
Howard, Ruth, 6,11,12,20
Howard, Wink, 11,12,17,21,22,23,27
Huxley, Aldous, 15
Isherwood, Christopher, 15
Leigh, Vivian, 8
Lombard, Carole, 30
Maugham, Somerset, 15
Nicholson, Harold, 15,31
Oberon, Merle, 11,12
Olivier, Laurence, 1,20,27
Pascal, Gabriel, 11,12
Selzneck, David O., 11,30
von Podewils, Baroness, 21
Walde, Alfons, 13

4) Characters in Shakespeare plays based on real people

Claudius, 18,22,26
Desdemonia, 14
Gertrude, 4,6,26
Hamlet, 2,4,5,6,7,8,9,17,18,19,20,22,23,25
King Lear, 5,25,26
Ophelia, 25,33
Othello, 14
Polonius, 4,25,33

Index to scenes in the screenplay
(names in parentheses are present in scene without speaking and/or only mentioned by speakers)

Scene 1 - Prologue - p. 41
Bette Davis, Howard, Goebbels, his wife

Scene 2 - New York, 1935 - p. 41
Howard, (Humphrey Bogart, Hitler)

Scene 3 - Hollywood, 1935 - p. 42
Howard, Merle Oberon (man, mothers, Bogart, Hitler)

Scene 4 - New York, 1935 - p. 45
Howard, Bogart, actress, Ruth Howard, Wink, Doodie, fans

Scene 5 - New York, 1935 (same night) - p. 48
Howard, his family

Scene 6 - New York, 1935 - p. 48
Howard, Ruth, Oberon, Doodie, (Rudy Vallee)

Scene 7 - New York, 1935 - p. 51
Howard, Doodie, Oberon

Scene 8 - New York, 1935 - p. 52
Howard, students, Schuyler Watts, Ruth, (Hamlet, William Shakespeare)

Scene 9 - New York, 1935 - p. 54
Howard, Oberon, Wink, Ruth, Doodie (Hamlet, Ophelia, Gertrude)

Scene 10 - New York, 1935 - p. 57
Howard, Oberon, (Ruth)

Scene 11 - New York, 1935 - p. 58
Goebbels (on screen), Howard, Oberon, Ruth, (Shakespeare, Hitler, Napoleon)

Scene 12 - Stowe Maries (Howard's home, Eng.), 1935 - p. 61
Howard, his family, Bogart

230

Scene 13 - Hollywood, filming Petrified Forest, 1935 - p. 62
Howard, Bogart, director, actor, script girl, (Hamlet, Romeo, Gielgud, Shakespeare, Norma Shearer)

Scene 14 - Hollywood, filming Romeo and Juliet, 1936 - p. 64
Howard, John Houseman, Watts, (Shakespeare, Hamlet)

Scene 15 - New York/Boston, rehearsing Hamlet, 1936 - p. 66
Howard, Houseman, eight beautiful women, Vivien Leigh, John Gielgud, Watts, Ruth, actor, Oberon, David Niven, (King Edward, Mrs. Simpson, Doodie, Hamlet, Churchill, Gertrude)

Scene 16 - New York, Opening Night, November 1936 - p. 72
Howard, Ruth, children, man, woman, Gielgud, Oberon, Niven, (Hamlet)

Scene 17 - New York, Hamlet, Nov./Dec. 1936 - p. 75
Howard, Gielgud, driver, (Hamlet)

Scene 18 - New York, December 11, 1936 - p. 75
Howard, Ruth, King Edward (on radio), (Churchill)

Scene 19 - On tour (Kansas City, L. A., etc), 1937 - p. 76
Howard, Ruth, interviewer

Scene 20 - New York, 1937 - p. 78
Howard, Watts (Shakespeare, Hamlet, Bacon, Edward de Vere, Queen Elizabeth, Gabriel Pascal, Henry Higgins)

Scene 21 - London, winter 1938 - p. 80
Howard, Violentte Cunningham, Pascal, (Hamlet, Higgins, Shakespeare, Charles Laughton, Gabriel Pascal, Alexander Korda, Churchill, Oberon, Shaw, Anthony Asquith)

Scene 22 - London, winter 1938 - p. 85
Churchill, Anthony Eden, Korda, Howard, (Philip of Spain, Napoleon, Nelson, Hitler, Shakespeare, Jesus, King Edward)

Scene 23 - London, winter 1938 - p. 88
Howard, Watts, (Edward de Vere, Hamlet, Virgin Queen, Gertrude, Shakespeare)

Scene 24 - Austria, winter 1938 - p. 89

Howard, Pascal, Alfons Walde (Goebbels, Doodie, Violette, Ruth)

Scene 25 - London, filming Pygmalion, Mar. 12, 1938 - p. 92
Howard, Pascal, Asquith, Wendy Hiller, young man

Scene 26 - London, 1938 - p. 93
Howard, Violette (Bonnie Prince Charlie, Hamlet, Edward de
Vere, Shakespeare)

Scene 27 - Pinewood Studios, filming Pygmalion, 1938 - p. 94
Howard, Asquith, Pascal, Violette (Oberon, H. de Vere Stacpoole,
Hamlet, Edward de Vere)

Scene 28 - Stowe Maries, London, Paris, 1938 - p. 96
Howard, Ruth. Violette, (Hamlet)

Scene 29 - Sailing to United States, fall 1938 - p. 99
Howard, Ruth and children, Violette

Scene 30 - New York, traveling to California, fall 1938 - p. 100
Howard, Violette, (Ashley Wilkes)

Scene 31 - Los Angeles, Hollywood, fall 1938 - p. 102
Howard, David Selznick, (Niven, Ingrid Bergman, Ashley)

Scene 32 - Beverly Hills, Hollywood, fall 1938 - p. 103
Howard, Violette, Bogart, Bette Davis, (Katharine Hepburn, Gary
Cooper, etc.)

Scene 33 - Los Angeles, winter 1939 - p. 107
Howard, Ruth, Doodie, (Ashley)

Scene 34 - Hollywood, spring 1939 - p. 109
Howard, Violette, Vivien Leigh, Laurence Olivier, photographers,
Bogart, (Merle Oberon, David Niven, Charles Laughton, Hamlet,
Korda , Oxford, Shakespeare)

Scene 35 - Desert outside Los Angeles, spring 1939 - p. 112
Howard, Violette, (Ruth)

Scene 36 - New York, summer 1939 - p. 113
Howard, Watts, (Hamlet, Queen, Oxford)

232

Scene 37 - Traveling, Stowe Maries, August 1939 - p. 114
  Howard, family, Violette, Chamberlain (on radio), official,
  (Shakespeare)

Scene 38 - London, September 1939 - p. 117
  Howard, Eden

Scene 39 - London, September 1939 - p. 118
  Howard, Violette, (Hitler, Pimpernel)

Scene 40 - Stowe Maries, London, fall 1939 - p. 119
  Howard, Ruth, Wink, Doodie, Violette, (money people)

Scene 41 - Paris, London, winter 1940 - p. 121
  Howard, Violette, (Hitler, Korda, Merle, Hamlet, Oxford)

Scene 42 - Churchill home, morning - winter 1940 - p. 122
  Churchill, Clementine, (Howard, Shakespeare, Oxford, Hamlet,
  Queen, Lady MacBeth, Somerset Maugham)

Scene 43 - A dinner party, April 2, 1940 - p. 123
  Howard, Clementine, Randolph Churchill, Kenneth Clark,
  Somerset Maugham, (Hilter, Aldous Huxley, Auden, Isherwood,
  Shakespeare, Oxford, Jesus, Hamlet)

Scene 44 - Churchill home, later that week, April 1940 - p. 127
  Churchill, Clementine, (Shakespeare, Maugham)

Scene 45 - London, May 1940 - p. 127
  (Howard, family), announcer, Churchill, Petain, (Violette, Hitler)

Scene 46 - London, spring 1940 - p. 128
  Howard

Scene 47 - London, spring 1940 - p. 129
  Howard, Violette, Wink, Doodie, Churchill (voice over) (Prince
  Edward, Shakespeare, Oxford)

Scene 48 - Pinewood Studios, London, winter 1941 - p. 133
  Howard, Alfred Chenhalls, Mary Morris, Violette, (Clark Gable)

Scene 49 - Pinewood Studios, winter 1941 - p. 135
  Howard, Mary, Chenhalls, Violette, journalist, (Michael

Redgrave, Hitler, Hamlet, Oxford)

Scene 50 - Pinewood Studios, winter 1941 - p. 138
Howard, Mary, (Violette)

Scene 51 - London, May 1941 - p. 139
Howard, Mary, (Hitler, Rudolf Hess)

Scene 52 - Outside London, spring 1941 - p. 142
Howard, Violette, Nazi, Churchill, Clemertine, (Shakespeare, Oxford, man)

Scene 53 - London, spring 1941 - p. 143
Howard, Violette, Chenhalls, (Oxford, Shakespeare, David, Jesus)

Scene 54 - Berlin, spring 1941 - p. 144
Goebbels, aide, (Howard)

Scene 55 - London, spring 1941 - p. 145
Gielgud, Leigh, Olivier, Howard, Violette, Chenhalls, (Shakespeare, Oxford, Hamlet, Hitler, Fortinbras, Claudius, Quisling, Churchill)

Scene 56 - Berlin, summer 1941 - p. 147
Goebbels, aide, Howard, German Captain, (Christ, Thomas Mann, Mattise, Picassso, Churchill, God)

Scene 57 - London, summer 1941 - p. 149
Howard, Churchill, Eden, Lord Haw Haw (radio), first and second men, (Hess, Duke of Hamilton, Prince Edward, Goebbels, Mitchell, Hamlet, Shakespeare, Scarlet Pimpernel, Oxford)

Scene 58 - Denham Studios, London, winter 1942 - p. 153
Oberon, Niven, Howard, leading lady, Violette, cameraman, (Hamlet)

Scene 59 - London, summer 1942 - p. 155
Howard, Jack Beddington, (Hamlet, Goebbels, Lord Nelson, Ruth, Doodie, Violette, Him)

Scene 60 - Outside London, fall 1942 - p. 157
Howard, Violette, Chenhalls, doctor, nurse, Ruth, (Doodie, Oberon)

234

Scene 61 - Stepney, London, November 1942 - p. 161
Howard, Violette, Ruth, (Doodie, doctors, nurses, Hamlet, Ashley, Scarlett)

Scene 62 - Hotel near the hospital, November 1942 - p. 162
Howard, Ruth, (Doodie), matron

Scene 63 - Hotel near hospital, November 4, 1942 - p.163
Howard, Chenhalls, Ruth, Doodie

Scene 64 - London, several days later, November 1942 - p. 165
Howard, Doodie, (mother)

Scene 65 - Outside London, November/December 1942 - p. 167
Howard, Ruth, Doodie, Chenhalls, (Violette)

Scene 66 - Pinewood Studios, Dec. 1942/winter 1943 - p. 168
Howard, Chenhalls, Beddington, (Hamlet, Violette)

Scene 67 - London, winter 1943 - p. 170
Howard, Chenhalls, Beddington, (Hamlet, Bard)

Scene 68 - Outside London, winter 1943 - p. 172
Howard, Chenhalls, Ruth, (Eden)

Scene 69 - London, winter 1943 - p. 174
Howard, Eden, (Hamlet, Franco, Salazar, Countess von Podewils, Lord Nelson, Churchill, Korda, Napoleon)

Scene 70 - London, April 19, 1943 - p. 177
Howard, Chenhalls

Scene 71 - London, April 1943 - p. 177
Howard, Eden, (Hamlet, Francis Vere, Horatio, De Vere, King, Queen)

Scene 72 - Outside London, April 1943 - p. 181
Howard, Ruth

Scene 73 - Airport / travel / Lisbon, April/May, 1943 - p. 181
Howard, Chenhalls, steward, (Hamlet, Doodie, Shakespeare, Horatio)

Scene 74 - Madrid, May 1943 - p. 185

Howard, Chenhalls, bartender, Goebbels, (Oberon)

Scene 75 - Madrid, May 1943 - p. 188
Howard, Chenhalls, Walter Starkie, W. B. Israel

Scene 76 - Madrid, May 1943 - p. 189
Howard, Chenhalls, Starkie, Israel, (Parson, Countess Podewals)

Scene 77 - Madrid, May 1943, party - p. 190
Howard, Countess, Starkie, Chenhalls, (Duke of Alba, artists, literary people)

Scene 78 - Madrid, May 1943, same party - p. 193
Howard, Countess, (Hamlet, Count, Hess)

Scene 79 - Madrid, May 1943, same party - p. 196
Howard, Countess, (flamenco dancer, Oxford, Shakespeare, Starkie, Prince Edward, Hess, Hitlet, Churchill)

Scene 80 - London, June 1 1943 - p. 199
Junior and Senior military officers, (Howard)

Scene 81 - Lisbon, June 1, 1943 - p. 199
Howard, Chenhalls, Junior and Senior military officers, (Oxford, Hamlet, Franco)

Scene 82 - Lisbon Airport, June 1, 1943 - p. 200
Howard, Chenhalls, Israel, steward, official, Holmes, junior officer, (mechanic, de Vere, Queen Elizabeth, Southampton, Churchill)

Scene 83 - Berlin / London / Lisbon, June 1943 - p. 205
Eden, Churchill, (Goebbels, Howard, Oberon, Chenhalls)

Scene 84 - London, later in June 1943 - p. 205
Vivian, Gielgud, (Howard, Laszlo, Oxford, Shakespeare, Raoul Wallenberg)